"When you do

Amy looked down. [...] step. He was going to do it. He was really going to dunk her. And that water was ice-bucket cold. In an act of desperation, she flung her arms around his neck and buried her face against him. "Okay, lumberjack. I go down. You go down."

"Have it your way, Doc." With that, he plunged beneath the frigid water.

The chill shocked her. Struggling not to gasp—which could result in her swallowing one of the scaly creatures swimming below the creek's surface—she tightened her hold on Hal.

He released her legs and slipped his arms around her waist. Then, with her body clasped tightly against his, he brought her back up.

They stood a moment holding onto each other, trying to catch their breath. Then, drawing back, Amy raked the hair away from her face and scowled at Hal, who looked tremendously pleased with himself.

"Are you happy now?" she asked, trying to sound disgruntled. Not an easy thing to do with laughter bubbling up from her chest, threatening escape.

The merriment in his eyes faded. His gaze dropped to her lips, then rose again to her eyes. "Yeah, Doc," he answered, his voice husky. "I'd say I'm pretty happy right now."

GINA FIELDS is a lifelong native of northeast Georgia. She is married to Terry and they have two very active, young sons. When Gina is not writing, singing, or playing piano, among a hundred homemaking activities, she enjoys volunteering for Special Olympics.

Books by Gina Fields

HEARTSONG PRESENTS
HP262—Heaven's Child
HP289—The Perfect Wife

Still Waters

Gina Fields

Heartsong Presents

This book is dedicated to: Dr. David J. Cadenhead, Dr. Gregory V. Smith, and Dr. Everett H. Roseberry

Thanks for allowing me to take advantage of all those office visits when I asked and you so willing answered my research questions. (Warning: There will probably be more in the future.) But most of all, thanks for listening, sharing, and caring.

And a special thanks to Boyd Cantrell, for giving me the grand tour of his sawmill.

A note from the author:
I love to hear from my readers! You may correspond with me by writing: **Gina Fields**
Author Relations
PO Box 719
Uhrichsville, OH 44683

ISBN 1-57748-751-6

STILL WATERS

Cover illustration by Randy Hamblin.

PRINTED IN THE U.S.A.

prologue

Dr. Amy Jordan slipped into the quiet haven of her office at Mercy Pediatrics in Atlanta, Georgia. She closed the door and leaned back against it with a sigh of relief. She felt like she'd just tangled with a mama grizzly protecting her cub instead of a three-year-old boy with a one-inch laceration on his knee. It had taken three nurses plus herself to conquer the resilient tyke.

A strand of long blond hair had worked loose from her French braid and hung in her peripheral vision like a large wet noodle. She reached up and tucked the errant lock behind her ear.

Her stomach growled, reminding her she had missed lunch and it was now time for supper. Ignoring the complaint, she pushed away from the door. She still had at least one hour of dictation to do, then rounds to make at the hospital. Plus, she was on call tonight. Who knew when she'd sit down for her next meal?

She added the file she carried to the foot-high stack on the corner of her mahogany desk, then slumped down into the leathery softness of her chair. Rolling forward, she reached into her jacket pocket, but a knock on her office door stopped her short of pulling out the miniature recorder she used for dictation.

"Come in," she called.

The late-duty nurse stepped inside carrying yet another file. What was her name? Jennifer Something-or-other. Amy couldn't remember. The young woman hadn't been working at the clinic long.

"Dr. Jordan," the nurse said as she approached the desk, "I have Jessica Jones's mother on the phone. She brought Jessica in to see Dr. Cape earlier today for allergies, but she's still concerned about Jessica's cough."

Amy reached for the file. "Which line is she on?"

"One." Jennifer handed the file to Amy. "Do you need anything else before I go?"

"No, thank you." Amy smiled. "Have a good evening."

As the nurse left, Amy opened the folder and scanned Dr. Cape's notes. Jessica Jones was a perfectly healthy four-year-old except for some pollen allergies that were presently making her young life miserable.

Dr. Cape had prescribed a cough elixir and an antihistamine—exactly what Amy would have done. It appeared all she needed to do was reassure Mrs. Jones that her little girl was going to be fine.

Amy picked up the receiver and pressed the blinking button. "Mrs. Jones, this is Dr. Jordan. What can I do for you this evening?"

Mrs. Jones gave Amy a brief outline of Jessica's earlier visit with Dr. Cape, ending with, "I gave her half a teaspoon of the syrup as Dr. Cape instructed, but her cough isn't getting any better."

"How long has it been since you gave her that dosage?"

"Two hours."

Amy checked Jessica's weight on the growth chart in her file. "You can go ahead and give her another half teaspoon now and see if that helps. If it doesn't, then I'm on call tonight and I'll be happy to see her in the emergency room."

A brief silence filled with agonizing contemplation filled Amy's ear. Then the stress-weary mother sighed as though someone had unplugged a balloon of pent-up worry and frustration trapped inside her. "I suppose I should try the extra syrup and see what that does before bringing her in." She paused again then, in a voice still laced with uncertainty, asked, "Do you really think she'll be okay?"

"I really think she'll be fine."

"Okay," Mrs. Jones said with one final sigh. "Thank you, Dr. Jordan."

Amy still sensed a perplexing reluctance on Mrs. Jones's part to break the connection and almost told her to go ahead and bring Jessica in. But on second thought, she decided not to. Amy had already been approached once by the senior partners in the practice about overextending herself to her patients.

After once again stressing she'd be available throughout the night, Amy, a bit reluctant herself, hung up the phone.

A little over an hour later, after the stack of patient files had been moved from one side of her desk to the other, she switched off her recorder and slipped it back into her pocket.

Pushing away from her desk, she did a quarter-turn in her swivel chair, stood, and stretched. Massaging the back of her neck, she wandered to the wall of windows in her fifth-floor office. She peered out through the open slats of the blinds to the darkening world outside.

Skyscrapers lined Atlanta's midnight-blue horizon like stacks of mismatched building blocks. Raindrops from a steady May shower shimmered in the city's awakening glow. A red, green, and blue motel sign glistened up through the mist like a neon rainbow waltzing in a waterfall.

Amy crossed her arms and leaned with one shoulder against the windowpane, a deep sense of serenity stealing over her. After what felt like a lifetime of hard work and study, she was finally a practicing pediatrician. That, in itself, would have been enough for her. But being asked six months ago to join the Mercy Pediatrics team, the largest, most successful pediatric practice in Atlanta, made obtaining her goal that much sweeter. Like an Olympic athlete going for the bronze but winning the gold instead.

And she'd done it without the influence of her father's name or money.

Amy's father, Dr. Nicholas Jordan, was one of the most sought after neurosurgeons on the east coast. He'd made quite a reputable name for himself—not to mention a substantial fortune—in the operating room. But Amy had never used his affluent credentials to boost her career. She wanted the satisfaction of knowing her accomplishments were her own. So, she had paid her tuition with scholarships, educational loans, and part-time jobs she'd picked up whenever her schedule permitted.

An ear-piercing *beep, beep, beep* shattered her moment of reflective silence. She swept back one side of her jacket and pressed a button on the pager attached to the waistband of her slacks. The hospital number flashed across the screen. She hurried to her desk, picked up the phone, and dialed. The answering nurse immediately transferred her to the resident on duty.

"Dr. Jordan, this is Dr. Kelly," the young man said. "I've got Jessica Jones in the emergency room. Her mother said she spoke with you an hour or so ago."

"That's right." Amy wasn't surprised Mrs. Jones had decided to bring in her daughter. She opened her bottom desk drawer and reached for her purse, readying herself to make the trip across the street to the hospital.

"She was brought in by ambulance a few minutes ago and it doesn't look good."

Amy stopped short of grasping her purse. "Ambulance?"

"Yes."

"But when I spoke with Mrs. Jones earlier, Jessica was only having trouble settling down from her allergies."

"Well, her asthma is complicating things now."

Amy frowned in befuddlement. She hadn't seen anything in Jessica's file about asthma. "What did you say?"

Dr. Kelly repeated his last statement, confirming Amy hadn't heard wrong. "Her breathing is becoming more labored by the minute," he added. "She's on the verge of respiratory arrest."

Amy clamped the receiver between her ear and shoulder and shuffled through the files on her desk, pulling out Jessica's. "Treatment so far?"

While Dr. Kelly spoke Amy searched frantically for documentation indicating Jessica had asthma. The folder should have been flagged so that anyone picking it up would know right away that the child had a potentially serious condition. It wasn't.

"But nothing I've tried is helping," Dr. Kelly finished.

Then, as though guided by a light beam in the darkness, her gaze fell on Jessica's birth date, and a wave of uneasiness rolled down her spine. "Jessica Jones" was a common name among young girls. Almost as common as "John Smith."

In a voice as calm as she could manage, she asked, "How old is this child?"

"Two."

His single word confirmed what Amy most feared—she'd been given the wrong file.

Stark reality slapped her with a battering force. The room swayed. Her legs almost buckled. She grasped the edge of her desk to keep from collapsing. *Oh, dear God, what have I done?*

"Dr. Jordan?"

The panic in Dr. Kelly's voice jerked her out of her shock-induced paralysis. She swallowed the lump in her throat that was threatening to smother her. "I'm on my way."

She slammed down the phone and fled her office. She repeatedly punched the elevator button while verbally attacking the passenger cart for being too slow. She raced across the crowded city street, ignoring the blaring car horns and blatant curses angry drivers flung out their windows at her.

"Dear God, please let me reach her in time," she prayed as she sailed through the swinging emergency room door.

She sprinted down the long hospital corridor, brushing past doctors and nurses trying to sidestep her path.

But in spite of her frantic efforts, and her desperate plea, Amy reached little Jessica Jones one heartbeat too late.

one

Three Months Later

This has been a good day.

Amy navigated her red sports convertible around another hairpin curve in the narrow road threading through southeastern Kentucky's Cumberland Gap Mountains. The earthy scent of the roadside soil and foliage awakened her senses to the untainted beauty surrounding her. Towering pines and mammoth hardwoods curtained each side of the thin highway, providing a leafy frame for the azure sky. The sun-dappled macadam carpet rolled out before her emitted a sense of tranquillity.

She reached over and popped a cassette into the car's tape player. One of her favorite easy listening tunes floated through the air.

Yes, this has been a good day, she told herself once more. *Better than yesterday. Better than the day before.*

A fading green sign attached to a rusting metal pole read "Cedar Creek, 5 miles." Amy smiled. What would Robert and Linda think when she showed up on their doorstep unannounced?

The doctor and nurse couple had moved from Atlanta to Cedar Creek two years ago to open a much-needed medical clinic in Linda's economically repressed hometown. Since that time, they'd extended many invitations to Amy, but it seemed like she was always too busy, too pressed for time to fit in a visit to her two best friends from college.

But not anymore. Now, at the ripe old age of thirty, she was a lady of leisure with nothing but time on her hands. She held onto her smile even as she felt the joyless lump rise in her throat.

10

Think positive thoughts, she reminded herself. Isn't that what her therapist had instructed her to do?

As she rounded the next curve, the car's engine sputtered. A ripple of panic flitted through her. "Oh, no. Don't quit on me now." As she uttered the words, the motor coughed twice more. She barely managed to pull the two right tires off the narrow road before the engine died completely.

Releasing an annoyed sigh, she scanned the instrument panel, trying to recall if any warning lights had come on. She knew virtually nothing about automobiles, except that they were made to be driven.

When her gaze fell on the fuel gauge, she stared at the gas hand resting below the "E" for a disparaging moment, and then her eyes slid shut. She shook her head. "Stupid, Amy. That's what you are. Stupid, stupid, stupid!" She'd passed scads of service stations on the expressway before taking the Cedar Creek exit. Why hadn't she thought to stop for gas before entering such a sparsely populated area?

She shifted into park and switched off the ignition to the dead motor. Then she dug her thin cellular phone and address book out of her purse and looked up Robert and Linda's telephone number. Flipping open the phone, she started to punch in the number but paused with her forefinger a mere inch above the first digit. The words "No Service" blinked at her from the digital display screen. Her dampening spirits plunged like a lead weight to the pit of her stomach. The area was apparently too mountainous to make a connection.

Slapping the phone shut, she crammed it and the address book back into her purse. She'd have to walk the rest of the way. Not a pleasant thought considering the heat and humidity of the late August afternoon.

She raised and secured the top of the car and locked the doors. Then, slinging her thin purse strap over her shoulder, she set out for Cedar Creek.

Around yet another sharp curve, she met with the remains of a tree that had been cut out of the road. A dense scattering of brown leaves still dangled on its gnarly branches. She side-stepped a large rock and lumbered over several limbs. When she was halfway across the last bough between her and the main trunk, a high-pitched buzz rose and reverberated through the air.

She froze, a chill of apprehension coursing her spine. Glancing down, she found the source of the sound and fought to keep her legs from buckling. Next to the tree trunk, less than three feet from her unprotected ankle, lay a large, coiled rattlesnake. The serpent's tail beat the air so fast it merely blurred. Its forked tongue darted in and out of its triangular head like scarlet streaks of lightning.

Amy stood stock-still, even though blood raced through her veins at record breaking speed. She knew if she moved she risked a bite. On the other hand, how long would it take the snake to lose interest in her and slither away? She decided she didn't have the nerve to find out.

Keeping her gaze fixed on the snake's black eyes, she withdrew her foot degree by degree. As her sole floated over the height of the branch, the rattler hissed.

Without further thought, Amy turned and fled, scaling the scattered logs as fast as her legs would carry her. Just when she thought she'd escaped to safety, the toe of her tennis shoe snagged a limb.

Ground and rock flew up to meet her. A piercing pain shot through her head. Then nothing.

%

Hal Cooper shifted his logging truck into third gear. The vehicle hesitated, groaned under its cumbersome burden, then continued plugging along at its own leisurely speed.

Hal hunched his shoulders and tilted back his head in an effort to ease the tension building in his neck. He'd hauled timber since he was sixteen. Half his life. He'd traveled every single roadway carved into these mountains, and few he found intimidating—including this one. But on this particular day, pulling his bulging load over this desolate route was proving to be a ruthless test of patience.

The sun bowing toward a craggy mountaintop reminded him what a long day it had been. His right-hand man had called in sick that morning. He'd spent his lunch hour delivering his newest truck to the mechanic—for the second time in two weeks. And that afternoon, another truck had suffered a broken chain and a flat tire.

He shifted gears again as he approached a sharp curve. Thank goodness tomorrow was Saturday. He'd reserved the entire day for his five-year-old daughter and fishing.

When he rounded the embankment, his grip tightened on the steering wheel.

"What the—?"

He swerved, barely missing a red convertible sitting half in, half out of the road. Once he cleared the automobile, he glanced in the mirror attached to the passenger door. A disgruntled frown marred his forehead. Only an imbecile would leave their car parked in such a dangerous place.

Around the next bend, he found that "imbecile" in the form of a woman lying beside the road in a crumpled heap.

Adrenaline kicked in, sending a spasm of alarm through his chest and moisture to his palms. He pulled his truck and trailer off the road as far as possible, set the emergency brakes, and switched on the hazard lights. Jumping out of the truck, he reached under the seat for the first aid kit.

A short sprint took him to her. She lay on her side, her head close to a large rock. Thick, dark-blond hair, secured by a green scarf at the nape of her neck, fanned out over the ground behind her. Long, slender arms and legs extended in all different directions from the green T-shirt and white shorts she wore. A thin leather purse strap looped the crook of one elbow.

Kneeling, he checked her pulse and breathing and found both strong and steady. He inhaled deeply, then exhaled slowly. This was a first for him. As a volunteer firefighter, he'd had emergency training and, a few times, rescued people and animals from burning buildings. But he'd never run upon anyone unconscious in the middle of nowhere.

Pursing his lips, he looked up at his truck and contemplated his next move. He had a cellular phone, but little good that would do in a "No Service" area. He glanced up and down the road, but with little hope. Who knew when someone would come along on this scarcely traveled route?

His gaze slid back to the unconscious woman. He'd have to move her, regardless of the risks.

Fighting the stubborn sense of trepidation stealing over him, he closed his eyes. "Dear Lord, please guide my hands. Let me not make one move that will cause this lady further injury."

Opening his eyes, he set aside the first aid kit and slipped the purse strap from around her elbow. Gently, he straightened her arms and legs, checking for broken bones. Fortunately, he found no evidence of any.

Holding his breath, he turned her onto her back. When her head bobbled from one side to the other, his chest contracted. An inch-long wound gaped open on the right side of her forehead next to her hairline. A droplet of blood oozed from the cut and trickled across her temple, spreading a crimson stain into her honey-gold hair. Gooseflesh raced down Hal's arms despite the warmth of the late summer day.

He wiped his wet palms on the thighs of his jeans before reaching for the latch on the emergency kit. After cleaning his hands with an antiseptic towelette, he withdrew a thick gauze wrap and a roll of white tape. With shaky hands, he cleansed her wound with antiseptic and applied a tight bandage. Then he sat back on his heels and allowed his gaze to linger a brief moment on the woman's striking features.

She was young, probably in her late twenties. She wore little, if any, makeup, but she needed none. Her tanned complexion was naturally smooth and unblemished. A small straight nose and full pink lips graced her delicate oval face. Thick, tawny lashes curled against slightly sun-kissed cheeks.

Clearly, God had been generous when He passed her way handing out physical assets.

Setting his mind back to the task at hand, he pulled a packet of smelling salts from the white box. He squeezed the tube, plastic crackled, and ammonia permeated the air. Then, leaning forward, he eased his free hand beneath her head. "Okay, Sleeping Beauty. Here we go."

&

A sharp, burning sensation seared Amy's nose and throat. She coughed, and an excruciating explosion ripped through her head. Wincing, she stilled herself against the pain.

"Ma'am, can you hear me?"

The softly spoken words penetrated her subconscious, pulling her up out of the black void she had fallen into. Slowly, she opened her eyes to a fuzzy world. As she blinked away the fog, a ruggedly handsome face materialized above her. A pair of piercing brown eyes peered down at her from beneath a brow creased with an unreadable frown.

Who in the world was this man? Someone she should know? His chocolate-colored hair was barely long enough to part and comb over to one side, and a dark five o'clock shadow shaded his dimpled chin and wedge-shaped jaw. His lips were drawn into a thin line.

To her dismay, she found nothing familiar in his aristocratic features.

The faint scent of sawdust mixed with the pungent odor of antiseptic wandered into her muddled senses, and she realized the stranger pillowed the back of her head in his hand.

Fear quickened her pulse. She curled her hands into tight fists. Grit imbedded underneath her fingernails. "Wh–who are you?"

He smiled, and his grimacing features softened. "Hal Cooper," he said in a velvet-edged voice. "I found you alongside the road a few minutes ago, out cold. Apparently, you fell and hit your head on a rock."

Her gaze traveled downward, over wide shoulders and a

broad chest. When she read the words "Cooper Lumber Mill, Cedar Creek, KY" stitched on the pocket of his light blue shirt, where she was and what had happened came back to her like a whirlwind. She noticed an open first aid kit on the ground beside him, and her fear dwindled. Considering the kit, he probably was telling the truth. She relaxed her fists.

"What about you?" he asked. "Do you have a name?"

She swallowed and tried to wet her lips. Her throat and mouth were so dry. "Amy Jordan," she finally managed to croak.

"Can you tell me what happened, Amy?"

She let her eyelids slide shut against the pain behind them. "I was on my way to Cedar Creek to visit friends when my car ran out of gas. I started walking but ran into a snake. I tripped trying to get away."

"A snake?"

She nodded, once.

"Did it bite you?"

She heard the rise of panic in his voice and opened her eyes, meeting his concerned expression. "No," she assured him. "Just scared me half to death."

"Do you know what kind it was?"

"A rattlesnake."

"Where was it?"

She pointed toward the cut up tree. "Over there, next to those logs. . .on this side of the trunk."

"I'm going to go see if he's still there." Hal gently replaced the hand holding her head with her purse. For some reason, the small gesture for the benefit of her comfort touched her.

With her head elevated by her handbag, Amy could watch his progress. He carefully prodded and parted each branch in front of him, then made each step with cautious hesitation. So sleek and graceful was each movement, he could have been a mountain lion sneaking up on unsuspecting prey.

After a thorough search along the logs, he returned and kneeled back down beside her. "He's gone. You probably scared him as much as he did you."

"I hope so."

One corner of his mouth twitched in amusement.

"He hissed at me!" Amy added offensively.

He pursed his lips, Amy suspected, to keep from laughing out loud. And Amy silently berated herself for sounding so petty, as though she thought the snake had invaded her territory, not the other way around.

She raised her head and started to sit up, but immediately found her shoulders pinned to the ground by his hands.

"Whoa! Wait a minute," he said. "Where do you think you're going?"

She eased her head back down. "I was hoping you would take me somewhere to get some gas so I could get my car out of the road."

"Not so fast. You have a head injury."

"Head injury?" she repeated in a small voice, hoping she'd heard wrong.

He nodded. "You cut your forehead when you fell. But it doesn't look too serious, and you're plenty coherent." He gave a nonchalant shrug. "A few stitches and I'm sure you'll be fine."

His seemingly unconcerned gesture and calm tone gave her a tenuous sense of relief. She raised her hand to her forehead and her fingers came in contact with a thick gauze bandage.

"That's my menial work," Hal explained, tossing the roll of tape into the white box at his side. "Dr. Sanders will do a much better job."

She blinked. "Dr. Sanders?" she repeated. "Do you know Robert?"

Hal closed the first aid kit. "Yep." Without giving her a chance to respond, he leaned forward, slipped one arm under her shoulders, and the other under her knees.

"What are you doing?" she wanted to know.

"Carrying you to my truck so I can get you to the clinic."

"There's no need. I can walk." At five-ten and one hundred

thirty-five pounds, she considered herself no small burden for any man. But this one lifted her off the ground and into the cradle of his strong arms, it seemed, with little effort.

"My purse," she reminded him as her arm circled his muscular shoulders.

"I'll come back and get it."

He carried her to a large white logging truck with a long skeleton bed weighed down with a massive load of timber. He set her on her feet and supported her with one arm around her back while he opened the passenger door. He then held onto her waist while she climbed up into the cab.

Amy settled herself on the worn leather seat and found a spot for her feet on the gritty floor among several large wrenches and an empty soft drink bottle.

When he closed the door, the resounding clang shot into each ear and clashed head-on in the center of her aching head. She winced.

While Hal retrieved her purse and his emergency kit, she examined her surroundings with a touch of curiosity. She'd never seen the inside of a logging truck before. Beyond the items absolutely necessary to operate the vehicle, the cab possessed an AM/FM radio with a missing knob and an air conditioner/heater. A cellular phone and two orange grease rags lay beside her in the seat, and a trace of diesel fuel hung in the air.

Amy's gaze settled on a wallet-size picture of a little girl taped to the paint-chipped dash. An abundance of dark curly hair framed dimpling cheeks and sparkling blue eyes. The child looked to be about four years old. Who was she? Amy wondered. Hal Cooper's daughter?

The photo reminded Amy that most of her friends were married and had children of their own. Robert and Linda were expecting their first in November. In the past, Amy hadn't had much room in her life for romance, much less commitment. She couldn't even recall the last time she'd had a date.

Hal opened the door, set her purse in the middle of the seat, and scooted the first aid kit beneath it. "How's your head?" he asked, climbing into the cab.

"A little better." The pain had diminished to a dull throb.

"Good." He pressed in the clutch with his left foot and reached for the key. "I'll try to take it easy, but sometimes this old truck has a mind of her own. She may jerk us around a bit."

Amy nodded, a little amused that he spoke of the vehicle as though it were an obstinate female.

He cranked the engine and released the emergency brake. Amy prepared herself for a jolt. Good thing she did, too, because the truck bolted a couple of times before settling down and offering them a smooth ride.

Once they were well under way, Amy motioned toward the picture taped to the dash. "Is that your daughter?"

Hal glanced at the photo, a lazy half grin tipping one corner of his mouth. "Yeah. Her name's Krista. She just turned five, but thinks she's fifteen."

Amy could almost see his chest swell with pride, and a wistful longing settled deep inside her. Swallowing, she said, "She's beautiful. You and your wife must be very proud."

His smile waned. "Krista's mother died four years ago."

Amy immediately regretted her remark. "I'm sorry. I didn't mean to pry."

"You didn't." He shifted gears. "Say you know Robert?"

A quick change in subject, she noticed. Of course, he didn't want to be reminded of what was probably the most painful time in his life. How many times over the past three months had she detoured around an unpleasant topic?

"Yes," she replied. "Since high school. I met his wife Linda at Emory while she was studying to be a nurse there. Of course, that was before she and Robert married."

"So you, Robert, and Linda all went to the same college, right?"

"That's right. In fact, they're the friends I was going to see when I ran out of gas." A brief silence passed while he adjusted the air conditioner, then Amy added, "You apparently know Robert and Linda pretty well if you know where they attended college."

An easy smile tugged at his lips. "I've known Linda all my life. We're first cousins."

Amy looked at him a thoughtful moment, taking in the information.

He arched his brows. "Surprised?"

"A little, I guess. Although, I suppose I shouldn't be. I remember Linda saying once she was related to half the people in Cedar Creek."

"She is." He shrugged. "We both are." He pressed a red button anchored to a small metal pole in the center of the floorboard. The truck seemed to gain a second wind, picking up speed as it started up a sharp incline. "Are you a nurse, too?"

An ache that had become as familiar as Amy's mirrored reflection rose in her chest. "No," she rasped past the tightness in her throat.

She knew propriety demanded some sort of explanation follow her blunt answer, so she cleared her throat and said, "I used to work in a doctor's office, but that was a long time ago."

A lifetime ago, she added to herself. At least, that's what the last few months had felt like.

Fearing her feelings would show on her face, she turned her head and stared out the dusty window, hoping Hal would ask no further questions about her former vocation.

After several long seconds, Hal replied, "I see."

Amy closed her eyes against the bitter sting of unshed tears. *No, Mr. Cooper, you don't see.* And she wanted to keep it that way. That part of her life was history. Best leave it where it belonged—in the past.

She drew in a ragged breath. This wasn't turning out to be such a good day after all.

two

During the remainder of the trip, Amy made no effort to resuscitate her conversation with Hal. Fortunately, neither did he.

Had it been another place, another time, she might enjoy an amicable talk with the handsome lumberjack. But not right now. She was too close to losing control.

Her chin quivered. She bit her lower her lip to stop it. Just that morning she had resolved to put Jessica's death behind her and move forward. Yet, Hal's one innocent question, "Are you a nurse, too?" had reminded her of what she once had, and all that was lost in the space of a single heartbeat. Would she ever be able to put her life back into order? Would she ever find a way to escape the pain, the disappointment, the guilt that constantly nipped at her heels no matter how hard she tried to outrun it?

She struggled to focus on the present, the here and now. But after a few rebellious seconds, the mental scale holding her fragile thoughts in balance tipped to the negative side and her mind traveled back to that dreadful night, and the debilitating days that followed.

The morning after Jessica's death, Amy had gone to the senior partner at Mercy and explained what happened. Standing in front of his desk, her heart lodged in her throat, she'd asked him, "How am I going to tell Jessica's parents about this?"

"You're not," came his blunt reply.

"But—"

"But, nothing, Amy. If you tell that little girl's parents what happened, we could very well find ourselves saddled with a wrongful death suit. Now, I don't want that, and I know you don't."

Of course she didn't. But she also thought Jessica's parents had a right to know why their daughter had died.

"Look, Amy," Dr. Dayton continued, "we're doctors, but we're also human. Mistakes happen. Take my advice and put last night behind you. Don't think about it, don't discuss it with another soul."

Amy stood there in bewilderment. How could Dr. Dayton, her mentor, Mercy Pediatrics' lead doctor, treat a child's death with such indifference, especially one that should never have happened? "What about Jennifer? Shouldn't I tell her to be more thorough in obtaining patient information before pulling a file?"

"I'll talk with Jennifer."

Numbly, Amy nodded and turned to go. What other choice did she have? He was her senior partner. He'd hired her. He could just as easily fire her, and see that she never worked in another reputable clinic again.

"Amy?" Dr. Dayton's gravelly voice stopped her as she reached for the door. When she looked back, he added, "This conversation never happened." The underlying warning in his words rang clear. *Talk, and you're history.*

That evening, Amy noticed, Jennifer was gone.

In the days that followed, Amy tried to follow Dr. Dayton's advice and carry on with her practice as she had before. But more often than not, she found herself second-guessing every diagnosis, every decision she made. She spent evenings pacing her office floor, reviewing files of the patients she'd examined that day, worrying she'd missed something important, something vital to one's health. She arrived at work each morning fearing she'd hear another child had died because of a careless mistake she had made.

Her colleagues had tried to encourage her, tell her it was normal for a doctor to question their abilities after losing a patient, especially their first. They'd tried to assure her that, eventually, things would get better.

But things didn't get better. They only got worse until, one day, after examining another asthmatic patient, Amy collapsed. When she woke, she was in the hospital, suffering from exhaustion and a nervous breakdown.

In two weeks her therapist deemed her strong enough to return home, but she'd never found the strength, or the courage, to return to her practice.

That one small oversight had cost her everything she had ever dreamed of—and a little girl her life. When comparing the two, Amy knew she had paid a much smaller price.

"Well, here we are."

The lumberjack's smooth voice mercifully interrupted Amy's dismal thoughts. She took a deep calming breath and forced her mind back to the present.

Hal turned off the road and into a parking lot just beyond a sign that read, "Cedar Creek Medical Center." A solitary vehicle, a tan sport utility Amy recognized as Robert's, sat in front of a one-story brick building.

"Good," Hal said. "It looks like Robert is still here."

The clinic was smaller than Amy had imagined, but, she suspected, plenty big enough to serve the citizens of Cedar Creek. If memory served her correctly, they hadn't run upon a single traffic light in the small town they had just passed through.

Hal eased his truck to a stop, taking up one entire side of the parking lot. "Wait. I'll come around and give you a hand." After switching off the engine, he set the emergency brake.

While he got out of the truck and circled in front of the cab, Amy opened the door and twisted around so her legs dangled over the side of the seat. When she glanced down, her world tilted. She steadied herself by bracing a palm on each side of the door frame.

Hal stepped into her line of vision and looked up at her. "Are you okay? You look a little pale."

"I'm fine. I just didn't realize the ground was so far away."

His lips curved in understanding. "Put your hands on my shoulders, and we'll get you down."

She did as he instructed, and as he reached for her waist, she stretched one foot toward the step. When the sole of her tennis shoe touched the rubber-coated surface, her foot kept right on going. Before she could regain her balance, she slid off the seat and slammed into Hal's hard body. His arms closed around her in an instant.

Amy's mouth dropped open, but she couldn't think of a thing to say. The manly smell of salt and sweat and sun-baked skin seeped into her senses like water to a thirsty sponge. She felt the rise and fall of his chest with each breath he took. She noticed his brown eyes had little gold flecks in them.

"Are you all right?"

His question jerked her out of her stupefied state and she snapped her mouth shut. Sliding her hands off his shoulders, she pushed away, but the feel of his sinewy chest lingered on her fingertips.

Warmth crept up her neck and over her face. She glanced down, brushing her hands down her shirt and shorts in a pretense of straightening them. "I'm sorry," she muttered. "I slipped."

"That's okay. How does your head feel?"

In the wake of the jolt, the throbbing had increased. She felt like someone was using her forehead for a dart board, but didn't want to complain. Lifting her eyes to his, she forced a smile. "Fine."

"Let's get you inside." He bent to pick her up.

She placed a hand on his shoulder, stopping him. "Mr. Cooper, I can walk."

Straightening, he pinned her with a dubious look and, after a second's hesitation, said, "Are you sure?"

She nodded.

"Okay," he said, but his tone held a trace of uncertainty.

They started across the parking lot, but three steps into the trek, the clinic teeter-tottered. Amy stopped, reaching for her forehead.

In one smooth motion, Hal stooped and swept her up in his

arms. She didn't argue, just slipped her arm around his neck, closed her eyes, and rested her head against his shoulder. Above the pain, she was aware of firm stomach muscles rippling across her hip with each step he took.

She heard a door open and raised her head to find Robert stepping outside the clinic.

"Hal?" he said, his voice elevated by surprise. Then he yanked off his wire-framed glasses. "Amy?"

"In the flesh." She tipped her head toward a raw scrape on her knee. "What there is left of it."

Still holding the door open, Robert stepped to the side. "What happened?"

"She met up with a snake out on Bear Slide Hollow." Hal explained, breezing past Robert and into the clinic without breaking his stride. "She fell and hit her head on a rock trying to get away. I think she'll need a few stitches."

"Take her into room four. There's an X-ray machine in there."

Hal carried her into the room and eased her down on the examining table, taking care when he pulled his arms from beneath her.

"Got a pillow?" he asked as Robert entered.

"The cabinet beneath the bed," the doctor answered.

Hal bent, opened and closed a door, then came up with a pillow clothed in a startlingly white pillow case. Leave it to Robert to always consider his patients' comfort.

Gently, Hal slid his hand beneath her head and raised it enough to slip the pillow underneath.

She met his gaze, and he smiled. "How's that?" he asked.

"Good. Thanks."

Robert put on his glasses and washed his hands. Then, stepping up to the table, he reached for the bandage on her forehead. "Now, let's see how much damage you've done."

Amy flinched twice when the tape tugged at her hair.

"Is there anything I can do to help?" Hal asked, as though sensitive to her discomfort.

"Yep." Robert answered, examining the laceration. "First, I'm going to take a couple of X-rays to make sure she's not cracked anything important, then I'll need you to hold her head while I numb her. She hates shots."

Amy glowered at Robert, who, in turn, ignored her. Her fear of needles was not something she cared to have advertised, even if it was true. She could give a shot without batting an eye. But when on the receiving end, she had to lie down to keep from passing out.

Hal pointed his thumb over his shoulder. "Do I have time to make a couple of calls?"

"Sure." Robert tossed the bandage in the trash. "You can use the phone in my office."

Two X-rays revealed Amy had gotten by with only a minor concussion, nothing to be overly concerned about. When Hal returned, Robert was filling a syringe. The lumberjack stopped at the sink to wash his hands, and when he finished, Robert said, "Okay, Hal, you come around here and hold her head." He pumped a couple drops of medication into the air.

A sick knot twisted in Amy stomach. She closed her eyes and balled her fists in anticipation of the injection. She heard shuffling, then two callused palms, slightly damp from their recent washing, framed her face. In a few seconds, a biting sting shot across her forehead and temple.

After the pain subsided, Hal withdrew his hands. She felt the heat emitting from his body move from the top of her head to her side. Then his strong, work-roughened fingers captured her fist and wormed their way inside until his hand circled hers.

Amy didn't open her eyes, just allowed the methodical stroke of his thumb across the back of her hand to work its magic on her taut nerves. By the time Robert pulled the first stitch, the queasiness in her stomach was gone.

Twenty minutes and six stitches later, Amy, after taking a few trial steps down the hallway, walked out of the clinic on her own, despite the disapproval of the two men with her. She and Robert waited next to his car while Hal retrieved her purse from his truck.

She reached for the handbag when he held it out to her. "Thank you so much, Mr. Cooper. For everything."

"Hal, please. And you're quite welcome."

"Could I pay you for your time and trouble?"

He hooked his thumbs in his back pockets. "Oh, no. I didn't do anything anybody else wouldn't have done. I'm just glad I came along when I did."

"Me, too." She slipped her purse strap over her shoulder. "Well, I guess I've taken up enough of your time." Turning to Robert, she said, "I need you to take me to a station for some gas so I can get my car out of the road."

"Oh, yeah," Hal injected, drawing her attention back to him. "I almost forgot. I called the local mechanic here. He has a tow truck and is going to deliver your car to Linda and Robert's house a little later on this evening."

Amy brushed a windblown strand of hair away from her face. "That was thoughtful of you."

He shrugged off the compliment. "It was sitting in a dangerous place. I was afraid someone would hit it, or get hurt."

"Let me get the name of the mechanic so I can get a check to him before I leave tomorrow." She slipped her purse off her arm and slid her thumb beneath the front flap.

"Oh, no. It's already taken care of."

Pausing, Amy looked up. "I can't let you do that."

Again, he shrugged. "The guy owed me a favor."

"But you should save the favor for yourself. Not waste it on a stranger."

He started walking away backwards. "Take care of your head, Ms. Jordan."

"Amy," she corrected.

"Amy. It was nice meeting you." His gaze shifted to Robert. "See you at church Sunday. Tell Linda I said 'hey.' " With that, Hal turned and sauntered to his truck.

Amy watched as he circled the cab, climbed inside, and

fired the engine. She thought of the caring way he'd held her head and then her hand while Robert sewed her up, and a sad thought slipped into her mind. Tomorrow, she'd be leaving Cedar Creek. She'd probably never see the disarming lumberjack again.

She released a disheartened sigh. It was probably for the best. He struck her as someone she'd like to have as a friend, but her life was too messed up right now to involve anyone else in it. This way, she'd be left with a pleasant memory of his coming to her rescue. Hopefully, he would, too.

She pivoted to face Robert, who now leaned back against the passenger door of his vehicle with his arms and legs crossed. "Are you ready to go?" she asked.

Grinning as though he'd been reading her thoughts, he said, "I'm waiting on you." He pushed away from the car and opened the door for her. She slid inside.

When Robert took his place behind the steering wheel, he turned on the ignition and a warm but welcome blast of air rushed into the car's steamy interior. Then, instead of shifting into reverse and backing out of the parking space, as Amy expected, he sat back in his seat, clasped his hands in his lap, and stared straight ahead like a man with a heavy thought on his mind.

Amy leaned forward and peered at him. "Is something wrong?"

He shifted his gaze to her. "Amy, what were you doing out on Bear Slide Hollow?"

"I was on my way to see you and Linda, but I ran out of gas. You know the rest of the story."

His dark brows rose, arching above the rim of his glasses. "*You* ran out of gas?"

"That's right," Amy answered, although she understood his surprise. She was notorious for keeping her fuel tank above the one-quarter mark for those times when she got stuck in Atlanta traffic. She lifted her shoulders in a helpless gesture. "How was I supposed to know there aren't any gas stations out on

Bear Slide Hollow, or whatever the name of that road is?"

He didn't respond immediately, just continued looking at her like she was a puzzle with a piece that didn't fit. "Linda didn't tell me you were coming," he finally said.

"Linda didn't know."

"What do you mean, 'Linda didn't know'?"

"I mean, I didn't call and tell her I was coming. I just got up this morning and decided to come."

"Just like that?"

"Just like that," she confirmed.

"On the spur-of-the-moment, you got up this morning and decided to come and see me and Linda."

"Yes. What's so unbelievable about that?"

"Amy, you've never done anything spur-of-the-moment in your life."

"There's a first time for everything." She hoped her attempt at putting lightness into her voice sounded more convincing to him than it did to her.

Apparently it didn't, because he narrowed his eyes and studied her. His perceptive gaze told her he saw right through her cheerful charade.

Slowly, he shook his head. "No, Amy. Something's wrong. Something's happened since you got out of the hospital."

The oppressive weight bore down on Amy's chest. Yes, something had happened. She'd walked away from her career, her life.

Robert knew about Jessica's death. He and Linda had been the first persons she'd called that night. He also knew about the nervous breakdown. But he didn't know of her decision to quit practicing medicine.

Perhaps, subconsciously, that's why she had come to Cedar Creek, to tell her two closest friends in the world that she had left her practice. After all, she'd told her father, her partners at Mercy Pediatrics, and a couple of close acquaintances in Atlanta. There was no one else left to tell—at least no one that mattered—except Robert and Linda.

"Well," Robert jabbed at her non-response. "Are you going to tell me what's wrong?"

Amy drew in a deep breath and gave Robert what she hoped was a convincing smile. "Sure. I'll tell you. But let's wait until we get to your house, so I can talk to you and Linda together."

"Okay," Robert said, and shifted the car into reverse.

Amy turned and stared absently out the window. How would Robert and Linda react when she told them she'd had to turn away from everything she knew and loved? Shock? Bewilderment? Disappointment—like she had seen in the face of her father?

Thankfully, Robert had agreed to wait so she could talk to him and Linda at the same time. That way, she'd have to retell the unpleasant story only once more.

She tucked her right lower lip between her teeth. Then, maybe she could figure out what to do with the rest of her life.

☙

"We want you to come and work with us."

At Linda's comment, Amy paused, a piece of jam-covered toast halfway to her mouth. She glanced across the breakfast table at her petite, dark-haired friend. Last night, Linda and Robert had taken the news of Amy's leaving the medical field better than Amy had expected. At first, they had been surprised and, like everyone else, tried to convince her to "give it a little more time." When they finally realized she was adamant in her decision, they hadn't looked at her with disappointment, but with a sad, relenting expression of acceptance.

Or so she thought.

Now, here they were asking her to come and work with them. Amy's gaze shifted from wife to husband, then back to wife. "You mean at the clinic?" she asked, to make sure she had heard correctly.

Robert swept his plate aside and folded his forearms on the table. "Amy, Linda and I have been talking about hiring an office manager. When Hal brought you into the clinic last night, I was still there because I was trying to catch up on paperwork. Linda usually helps, but her doctor has ordered her to slow down. It's getting really hard for me to run the office now, and it'll be impossible when she takes maternity leave. Plus, I'd like to be able to spend my evenings with her and the baby instead of tied down at the clinic filling out orders for medical supplies."

Amy returned her toast to her plate and pushed it away. "Robert, I don't think I need to work in a clinic, much less be around patients, right now."

"You won't be around patients. Our receptionist makes appointments and answers the phone, and we've just hired another nurse. You'll have your own office, away from the waiting area. You'll be in charge of things like supply orders, payroll, and accounting. Basically, you'll see that the office is run smoothly and handle minor problems without the other employees having to come to me."

Amy leaned back in her chair, crossing her arms. "You can't be serious. I don't know anything about acquisitions and payroll."

Robert settled back and crossed his arms, matching Amy's position. "You're a quick study and have a lot of common sense. You'll do fine. Besides, if all goes well, Linda will have time to train you before the baby comes."

Amy glanced from Robert's staid expression to Linda's hopeful one. She couldn't believe it. They were serious.

With the fingertips on one hand, she rubbed her forehead in contemplation, wincing when she came in contact with the bandage on her head. Then she clasped her hands in her lap. "Look, guys, I don't know about this. I mean, I'm a city girl. I like the feel of concrete beneath my feet. I'm used to living next door to every modern convenience known to man. I don't know if I would be happy living here."

"Are you happy where you are now, Amy?"

The question came from Robert and pierced Amy's soul

like a flaming arrow. She met his perceptive gaze. Did he
mean geographic location or the pitiful state of limbo her life
was in? It really didn't matter, the answer to both questions
was "No."

Amy swallowed, fighting the onslaught of moisture pooling
in her eyes and making Robert look like an oblique, crystal-
lized blur.

"I'm sorry, Amy," he added, his voice full of remorse. "I
didn't say that to hurt you. But, I know you. We both do, and
only want what's best for you. You'll never be happy living an
aimless life. You know that." A fuzzy grin spread across his
tear-clouded face. "And, at the risk of sounding a little selfish,
we really could use your help right now."

Linda reached across the table and placed a warm hand
over Amy's. "Come on, Amy. It would mean so much to me
and Robert, having you here."

Amy blinked away the tears she had somehow managed to
hold at bay and studied the two people who were more like a
family to her than her own. They had always been there for
her, put up with her on holidays when her father had been too
busy to even call, encouraged her through medical school
whenever she felt like giving up. After her breakdown, they
had flown down and stayed with her those first few days she
was in the hospital, when she felt like she was broken into a
million pieces and her world would never be sane again.

And now they needed her. Maybe not as much as she
needed them, she acknowledged begrudgingly. But they did
need her. How could she refuse their request?

"You can stay with us," Linda offered in a small, earnest
voice.

Amy raised her hands in surrender. "Oh, all right. I'll help
out. At least until after Linda has the baby and gets back into
the swing of things. Then," she shrugged, "if I don't like it, I
suppose I can always quit."

A relieved smile stretched across Robert's face. "Great."

"I won't live with you guys, though. I want to find a place

of my own." Amy reached for her plate, pulling it back in front of her. "There's only one condition to this deal. I don't want anyone here to know that I am. . .*was* a doctor." She hesitated for a thoughtful second. "Or who my father is."

"Nicholas Jordan" had been in so many medical journals, he was practically a household name in the field of medicine. Who could say he wasn't known to someone in the Cumberland Gap region? For all she knew, he could have performed surgery on someone in the area.

"You mean you don't want anyone to know you're filthy rich," Linda said, training shrewd eyes on Amy.

Yes, Amy was wealthy, thanks to an early inheritance from her father. And more than once she'd wondered if her so-called friends—Robert and Linda excluded—were loyal to her, or her money. "Right," she said with conviction. "I want to be known as plain old Amy, Miss Average, for a change."

"Pardon, me, Sweetie, but that's two."

Amy arched chiding brows. "Promise, or I'm outta here."

"I promise," Robert said. "Besides, that might not be such a bad idea. The locals in this area tend to shy away from prosperity."

Good. She'd convinced Robert. But he understood her. They came from the similar molds. His own father had accomplished fortune and fame as a stockbroker. Now to convince Linda, who, bless her heart, wasn't all that good at keeping secrets.

Amy fixed her gaze on Linda, and an understanding smile tipped the nurse's lips. "I promise," she said, then propped her elbow on the table and her chin in her hand. "Now, about finding you a place to live. I know someone who just might have a rental house available."

"Who?" Amy picked up her toast and started to take a bite.

"My Aunt Ellen, Hal's mother."

At the mention of the lumberjack's name, a small tremor ran down Amy's arm to her fingertips, and a dollop a strawberry jam dribbled down her chin.

three

One week later, Amy sat cross-legged in the center of her new living room floor, surrounded by a semi-circle of four cardboard boxes. Three of these cartons held symbols of her future—new clothes to suit her new lifestyle and a few treasured books and compact discs. The other held remnants of her past—her physician's bag and medical degrees. Everything else she had donated to charity when she canceled the lease on her apartment.

She'd considered hanging onto the Atlanta condo in case things didn't work out in Cedar Creek, but, on second thought, decided not to. That part of her life was over. Why leave excuses to go back?

She glanced around the cozy room. Ruffled eyelet curtains added a crispness to the pale yellow walls, and a red brick fireplace offered a touch of nostalgia. Everything about the small rental house was quaint and charming, much more homey and unpretentious than anything she'd ever lived in before. To her surprise and delight, she liked it.

According to Linda, after Hal's wife died in a tragic plane crash, his mother had moved in with him in order to take care of his daughter during his long, unpredictable work hours. Ellen Cooper, Linda had said, firmly believed a child's life needed structure and solidity. A sense of belonging. She had willingly given up her home of thirty-something years in order to help Hal provide that for his daughter.

Amy agreed with the older woman's way of thinking, and thought it wonderful a family would pull together in the face of a crisis for the sake of a child.

A telephone rang, startling Amy out of her reflective daydream. Hand pressed against her chest, she whipped around and stared at the phone on the end table, where the sound had come from. She didn't know service had been connected. She'd arrived only an hour ago and hadn't had a chance to go by the telephone office. Since it was Saturday, she figured they'd be closed anyway.

Another jangle reverberated the air. Amy twisted and stretched her hand toward the receiver, interrupting the third ring. "Hello."

"Amy! I see you made it."

"Linda. I should have known that was you. Do you have any idea who had this telephone connected?"

"Robert did that a couple of days ago. You need to drop by the telephone office one day next week and sign the order."

"You mean they hooked it up without my signature?" Amy asked in disbelief. In Atlanta, a signature was required for everything.

"One of the benefits of living in a small town, dear."

"If you say so," was the only response Amy could think of. Using her free hand for leverage, she scrambled up off of the floor and onto a green and yellow floral-patterned sofa. Turning sideways, she stretched out her legs, crossing them at the ankles, and leaned back against the settee arm. How long had it been since she'd allowed herself to relax in such a way? She couldn't remember.

"Robert and I are asking a few friends over for supper tonight," Linda said. "Wanna come?"

"Sure. My cupboards are still bare. I haven't had a chance to check out the food markets yet."

"Market," Linda corrected. "There's only one grocery store here."

Amy looked heavenward and shook her head. Did this town have more than one of anything? "Does this market have a deli?"

"No."

Amy funneled her fingers through her hair. "Good. I guess that means I don't have to bring anything."

"Nothing except yourself. We'll eat around six."

"I'll be there."

❧

When Hal pulled into Robert and Linda's driveway that evening, he immediately smelled a rat—a matchmaking rat in the form of his meddling first cousin. Linda had phoned him at work that afternoon and invited him to supper, explaining she and Robert were having a few friends over to meet their new employee. But the only other vehicle in sight, besides Robert's SUV and Linda's compact sedan, was a little red convertible with a Georgia tag. Which meant, the only guest present besides him *was* their new employee.

He got out of his ten-year-old white pickup and ambled to the door. Eight days ago, when he'd driven away from the clinic, he thought he'd never see the green-eyed beauty again. Then, the next afternoon, his mother told him she'd rented her house to Robert and Linda's new office manager. "You'll never guess who it is," his mother had said.

"Who?" he'd asked.

"Amy Jordan. You remember, the young woman you found unconscious out on Bear Slide Hollow."

Yes, Hal remembered. Unusual circumstances of their first meeting aside, Amy Jordan was not a woman a man could easily forget—even if he wanted to.

And Hal wanted to.

She was too beautiful, too perfect on the outside to not have some serious flaws inside.

Just like Adrienne.

The thought flitted through Hal's mind unbidden. He just as quickly pushed it away. The last thing he wanted to think about right now was his deceased wife and their stormy four-year marriage.

The front door opened before he had a chance to knock. "Come in," his ever-buoyant cousin said.

He stepped inside and followed Linda to the kitchen, where she'd apparently been cutting vegetables for a salad. He glanced around the room. "Where is everybody?"

Linda, seven months pregnant, waddled to the sink and picked up a tomato. "Robert's gone to the store for more milk—we're having homemade ice cream for dessert—and Krista's keeping Amy busy in the backyard."

Since it was Hal's mother's weekend to sit with her sick aunt in Lexington, Linda had volunteered to keep Krista that afternoon so he could get in a few hours' work at the sawmill.

Hooking his fingers in the back pockets of his jeans, Hal traipsed to the bay window overlooking the backyard and there she was—the woman who had crossed his mind at least once every waking hour over the past eight days. She kneeled with her shoulder angled toward him, one arm draped loosely around his daughter's back. With her free hand she pointed toward a yellow butterfly on a wilting fuchsia crepe myrtle blossom.

She wore her tawny mane in a French braid that hung down between her shoulder blades. With each small movement she made, rays from the setting sun bounced off her crowning glory like a radiant halo. She tilted her head, giving Hal a shadowed view of her profile. But he didn't have to see her face to remember every delicate feature, each minor detail, right down to the tiny brown mole next to her left eye.

Amy was the kind of woman who stood out in a crowd. Hal knew; he'd seen it all before. She'd walk into a room and men would turn their heads in awe, women in envy. One coquettish smile from her could set a man's heart to racing. One sensuous touch could sear a man's soul and take possession of his God-given free will.

He noticed Krista studying Amy's hair and saying something. Amy looked at Krista, smiled, and said something back. Krista nodded and wrapped her arms around the woman's neck. Amy closed her eyes and returned the hug.

The scene kindled a spark of anger inside Hal. Of course, if Amy was in on Linda's matchmaking scheme, she'd try to gain his good graces by using his daughter.

Out of the corner of his eye, Hal saw Linda step up beside him.

"What do you think of our new office manager?" she asked.

Given his most recent ruminations, he chose not to answer her question. Instead, he looked down at her and asked a question of his own. "What happened to everyone else that was supposed to come?"

Linda crossed her arms over her extended middle. "Well, as you know, your mom's sitting with Aunt Lucille. My mom and dad had already committed to the senior supper at church. Bill, Judy, Jeff, and Debbie all had other plans. And Kip and Nancy weren't home when I called."

"Sounds convenient." He heard the hard edge in his voice, but couldn't help it. He didn't appreciate being taken for a fool.

Linda studied him for a moment with a blank expression, like she was searching for the meaning behind his comment. Then a quizzical frown wrinkled her forehead. "What's that supposed to mean?"

"Linda, I know a set up when I see one."

Her mouth dropped open in offense. "Is that what you think this is?"

"Kind of obvious, isn't it? I mean, out of all the people you were supposed to invite, the only two who showed were me and Amy."

Linda drew her lips into a thin line and her eyes flashed with fury. Perching her fists on her hips, she did a quarter turn and faced him squarely. "Hal Cooper, I'll have you know I did ask the others to come. Or, at least, I tried. If I were going to try and set you and Amy up, I might be a little sneaky about it, but I wouldn't tell a flat out lie."

Guilt pricked Hal's conscience. What Linda said was true. She had been guilty of trying to fix him up on blind dates before, but she'd never been dishonest about it. And she wouldn't be now.

His shoulders drooped. Suddenly he felt tired and weary

and wanted the evening to be over so he could go home. "I didn't mean to accuse you of lying. It's just that, the whole thing looks so. . .suspicious."

"Hal, all I wanted to do is introduce Amy to a few of our friends, let her get to know them. It just happened you're the only one who could make it."

"Okay. Point taken." He stepped around her and strode toward the door. "I think I'll go see my daughter."

"Hal."

He stopped with his hand on the knob and looked at her.

"Is something bothering you?" she asked.

"No. Why?"

"You're. . .I don't know. Not acting like yourself tonight."

"Nothing's bothering me, Linda. I guess I'm just a little tired. It's been a long day." He started to open the door.

"Hal."

He gave her a "What now?" look.

"I know you're tired, but would you please try to make Amy feel welcome? Life hasn't been so good to her lately, and she could use a good friend right now."

Hal wondered what Linda meant, but didn't ask. He didn't want to feel sorry for Amy Jordan. He didn't want to feel anything for her. "Of course, I'll make her feel welcome. What do I look like? A monster?" With that he pulled open the door.

"A grouch," he heard her say before he closed it.

"Daddy!" Krista yelled when she saw him.

He lumbered down the deck steps and kneeled on one knee just in time to catch her. "Hey, Buttercup. How's my girl?"

"Doin' good, Daddy." She circled his neck with his arms and squeezed. Just as quickly, she pushed away, planting an enthusiastic kiss on his cheek. With her tiny hands resting on his shoulders, she looked at him through huge blue eyes alight with youthful exuberance. "Daddy, Amy said she would fix my hair like hers tonight."

Hal tugged on one of his daughter's dark, curly pigtails. "You mean 'Miss Jordan,' don't you?"

"I told her she could use my first name," Amy said from where she'd stopped a few feet away. "It doesn't bother me, if it doesn't bother you."

He slanted her a glance, then focused his attention back on his daughter. "Well, it was very nice of Miss Amy to offer to fix your hair like hers, but it'll have to wait until after supper. I think Aunt Linda's about got everything ready, and you need to wash up." Even though Robert and Linda were actually Krista's second cousins, the child had always referred to them as Uncle Robert and Aunt Linda.

Her cherubic cheeks dimpled. "Okay." She skipped away like a dandelion dancing in the wind, her pigtails bouncing along behind her.

As Hal stood, Amy took a couple of steps forward. He noticed the stitches were gone from her forehead, and her wound appeared to be healing well.

"It's nice to see you again, Hal," she said, extending her right hand. "I didn't get a chance to thank you for having my car filled up before you had it delivered here last week."

Her hand was soft and smooth, but her grip firm and confident, like she'd made the move a thousand times over. She was, Hal gathered, comfortable greeting people.

"I hope you'll allow me to reimburse you for the expense," she added, releasing his hand.

Hal expected to find something beguiling in her smile, something intentionally provocative in her stance. But all he saw was open friendliness coupled with a touch of decorum—and class. Hal recognized class when he saw it. And Amy Jordan had it.

"No, Miss Jordan," he said. "I'll not allow you to reimburse me. I was just glad I could help. How's your head?"

She blinked, her smile faltering at the formal use of her name. "Fine. Much better than a week ago. Thanks."

He tucked his thumbs in his back pockets. "Did you find everything okay at the rental house?"

"Yes, I did." She stuffed her fisted hands in the front pockets of her jeans. "The house is charming. I think I'm going to enjoy living there."

"I'm glad to hear that. If you need anything or any problems come up, just let me or Mom know."

"I will." She trapped the right side of her lower lip between her teeth and studied him a silent moment, her expression turning serious. Then, releasing her lip, she said, "Hal, have you noticed the bruises on Krista's arms?"

The unexpected question caught him off guard. His brow dipped. "Of course, I have," he said, biting back a sharp retort. "She's my daughter."

A frown Hal read as concern creased her smooth forehead. "Do you have any idea how she got them?"

"Probably playing. She's a very active little girl."

A timid smile tipped her lips, but her countenance remained solemn. "I see."

Hal narrowed his eyes. He wasn't sure he liked where her line of questioning was headed. "Why do you ask?"

"Because the bruises don't look normal. Not like those a child would receive as a result of everyday play."

He cocked his head to one side. "Just what are you trying to say?"

"That maybe Krista's bruises should be checked out by a doctor to determine exactly what caused them."

"How do you know they haven't been checked out by a doctor?" came Hal's quick response, then he clamped his mouth shut. The welfare of his daughter was none of Amy's business.

His rational mind told him to turn and walk away before he lost his temper, but his already wound up emotions got the best of him. His breathing became labored. He unhooked his thumbs from his back pockets and curled his hands into fists at his sides to keep from pointing a finger in her face. "Let me tell you something, Miss Jordan. When Krista's not with me, she's with my mother or, on a rare occasion, Linda. And none of us are child abusers."

Amy didn't flinch. "I didn't imply that you were."

His eyebrows shot up. "Didn't you?"

Her expression remained steady, unreadable. "No, Hal, I didn't. I merely suggested you have her checked out by a doctor."

He stared at her a dumbfounded moment. "What are you? Some kind of child care expert who thinks she can look at a bruise and tell what made it?"

She closed her eyes and ran her fingertips across her forehead, like she was counting to ten. Then, opening her eyes, she tucked her hand back into her jeans' pocket and released a long, slow sigh. "No, Mr. Cooper. I'm no expert."

"Then I think you should keep your opinions concerning my daughter to yourself." With that, he turned and stormed to the house.

When he stepped inside, Linda took one look at him and said, "I take it that didn't go well."

"That, my dear cousin, is an understatement." He scanned the room and found no sign of his daughter. Turning toward the bathroom, he yelled, "Krista, let's go!"

❧

"Hal did bring Krista into the clinic about a month ago," Robert told Amy after she explained what had transpired between her and Hal earlier. "He expressed concern over some bruises on her back. I did a full work up on her, and everything checked out fine."

Amy, Linda, and Robert had been sitting at the couple's dinner table for ten minutes, but Amy hadn't touched her food.

"Did you do a complete CBC?"

"Yes."

Amy didn't know what was driving her to question Robert. She knew he was an excellent physician. "Platelet count, red blood count, and white blood count were all normal?"

"Lymphocytes. Everything. I even sent her to a specialist in Lexington. He didn't find anything either. He concluded Krista had to be receiving the bruises during her playtime. She is pretty much a tomboy."

Amy pursed her lips. She'd already figured out Linda and Robert adored Hal and his family. She didn't want to ask her next question, but her conscience wouldn't let her keep it to herself. "Hal. . .or his mother. . .would never. . ."

"No," came Linda's quick answer. "In fact, when it comes to discipline, Hal could use a little firmer hand. And his mother? A child has never been blessed with a better grandmother."

Amy felt all her old insecurities closing in on her, feelings she thought she'd left behind in Atlanta. She ducked her head and fiddled with her napkin.

"Why don't I have Hal bring Krista into the clinic and you do a workup on her?"

Robert's question brought Amy's head up. "You know I can't do that."

"Why not? You still have a license."

"I can't practice medicine anymore, and tonight was a perfect example why. I second-guess and question everything. I'm suspicious of the most innocent circumstances. Besides, Hal thinks I accused him of child abuse, and, in a way, maybe I did. I'm the last person on earth he'd want examining his daughter."

Robert studied her for a pensive moment. "But I get the feeling your instincts are telling you something's been missed."

"My instincts can no longer be trusted, Robert." She pushed away from the table. "I'm sorry, but I'm not really hungry right now." She lumbered to the front door, retrieving her purse from a nearby hall tree.

"Wait a minute," Linda said. "Where are you going?"

She stopped and looked back. Robert and Linda were both standing, a befuddled expression on their faces.

"I'm going to apologize to Hal," Amy said. "And then, I have a feeling I may be looking for another place to live."

four

Hal lived just two curves—one-quarter mile—away from Amy. The rugged Cumberland Gap Mountains, silhouetted by the setting sun, provided a picturesque background for his two-story brick house with its wraparound porch.

Amy parked in front of the two-car garage and, upon stepping out of her car, was greeted by a friendly golden Labrador retriever. Stooping, she rubbed the dog behind his ears, noting the identification tag on his collar read *H. Cooper,* then listed an address and telephone number.

"Hi there, fella. Is your owner home?" Since the garage doors were closed, Amy had no way of knowing if Hal's vehicle was inside.

The canine, apparently pleased with her attention, jutted his nose forward. Amy saw what was coming and jerked back her head, barely dodging the dog's tongue. "Oh, no, you don't," she said with a laugh. "You're a handsome guy, but no kissing on the first date." Giving the dog one last tousle on his head, she added, "I'd like to hang around and play a game of fetch with you, but, right now, I really need to talk to your master."

She stood, tucking her hands into the pockets of her green sports jacket. Strolling up the curving walkway leading to the front porch, she wondered what kind of reception she'd receive. At this point, she didn't know what to expect from the handsome lumberjack. Thinking back to eight days ago, it was hard to believe he was the same gentle-natured man who'd so tenderly held her hand while Robert sewed up her head.

Her mind sprang forward to today and the first few minutes of their meeting in Robert and Linda's backyard. Even before she'd approached him about his daughter's bruises, Amy sensed a guarded wariness about him. The moment he first referred to her as "Miss Jordan," she'd gotten the feeling he was draw-ing a boundary line between them and daring her to cross it.

She climbed the two wide brick steps leading up to the porch. Maybe her first impression of him had been wrong. Maybe he wasn't someone she would want as a friend after all.

A touch of irony tipped her lips when she stepped onto the "Welcome" mat. Just how *welcome* would she be?

"No time like the present to find out," she muttered. Taking a deep breath of courage, she rang the bell. Slipping her hand back into her jacket pocket, she straightened her spine and prepared herself for whatever.

She waited only a few seconds before the overhead porch light came on and the doorknob rattled. Then Hal's voice, out-lined with a rough edge, spilled out of the yawning opening.

"Okay, Linda, if you came to tell me what a jerk I acted like tonight, I already—" He stopped short when he saw it was not his cousin, but Amy on the other side of his threshold.

Hand still grasping the doorknob, he stood transfixed in the luminous glow of the porch light, his face frozen in an unguarded expression of surprise. He'd untucked his blue and red plaid shirt from the waist of his blue jeans, and his short brown hair appeared at bit unruly, like he'd recently run his fingers through it.

For an instant, Amy sensed she was catching a glimpse of the real Hal Cooper, the one who'd picked her up off the side of the road last week and driven her to the doctor. The one who'd held her head while Robert gave her the shot. The Hal who'd stayed beside her, holding her hand, while Robert pulled the stitches. The same man considerate enough to have gas put in her car before having the vehicle delivered to her friends' house.

Amy opened her mouth to greet him, but the words got stuck in her throat along with her breath. The sudden manly aware-ness of him scattered her common sensibilities in a dozen dif-ferent directions. Her purpose for being there temporarily deserted her.

Then he blinked, and whatever had cast the entrancing spell

over her dissipated like a warm vapor in a cold wind. His guard came back up as quickly as his surprise had fallen over him when he first opened the door and found her standing on his front porch.

As though summoned by the chilly atmosphere, a cool breeze stirred, brushing Amy's flushed face. She reached up and tucked the wayward strand of hair that was always working loose from her French braid behind her ear.

"Hello, Hal," she said, breaking the expanding silence between them.

He braced his free hand on the door frame as though barring her from entering. "Miss Jordan." He nodded curtly.

"I was wondering if I could speak with you a minute."

At first he didn't respond, merely studied her with an indefinable expression.

Amy was beginning to think he was going to refuse her request and ask her to leave when he finally stepped back and motioned for her to come inside.

As she walked past him, the essence of soap and man, a pleasant scent undisguised by cologne or aftershave, wrapped around her senses.

She padded through the foyer to the living room where a hunter green leather sofa with a matching recliner flanking each side faced a rock fireplace. She stopped in the center of an Oriental rug spread over the hardwood floor and scanned the room. "You have a lovely home."

"Thank you, Miss Jordan. But I'm sure you didn't—"

She pivoted to face him. "You're right. I didn't come here to talk about your house, or your daughter. I came to apologize."

He studied her with a look of skepticism, like he was checking and rechecking her words to see if he could find a hidden motive or an unscrupulous meaning behind them.

Swallowing, she continued. "When I questioned you about Krista's bruises, I stepped over a line I had no right to cross. It won't happen again." *Maybe* a stubborn sector of her conscience whispered.

In spite of Robert's logical explanation for Krista's bruising, Amy could not quell the gut feeling telling her something was still amiss where Krista was concerned. In the past, Amy had depended on that internal instinct whenever she was dealing with an out-of-the-ordinary case. The only time she had chosen to ignore it, a little girl had lost her life. An alarming thought spurred Amy's conscience. Was she making that same mistake again?

Hal shifted his weight, tucking his thumbs into his back pockets. The movement jerked Amy out of her musings, and she reminded herself—for about the tenth time that evening—she was no longer practicing medicine. Even if she were, Krista would not be her patient but Robert's. Amy knew the little girl was in capable hands.

"You've apparently talked to Robert," Hal said.

"Yes. But that still doesn't excuse the way I approached you this evening."

Hal brushed a hand down over his face, then hooked that same hand around the back of his neck. The action seemed to wipe away his cryptic edginess, leaving behind a very weary man.

Shoulders drooping, he said, "I think I owe you an apology, too, Miss Jordan. I was in a foul mood when I got to Linda's this evening, and I'm afraid I took my frustrations out on you. I'm sorry. I shouldn't have lost my temper."

Amy was lost for an immediate response. He was like the wind during the changing of seasons: warm one minute, cool the next. And right now he was once again showing her the side of him she wanted to know a little better, learn more about.

Suddenly, she felt a magnetic pull toward him and an overwhelming urge to step forward, reach up and lay a comforting hand on his wedge-shaped jaw, feel the roughness of his five o'clock shadow. But prudence prevailed and she quelled her overactive emotions, which seemed to be struggling to go in a direction that contradicted Amy's usual levelheadedness.

Hal Cooper was an avenue Amy couldn't afford to explore right now. She was in Cedar Creek to start a new life, not make friends who might ask questions about her old one.

Reminding herself she'd done what she came to do and it was now time to go, she said, "Thank you for understanding. I suppose I've taken up enough of your time."

A door to Amy's right swung open and Krista walked into the room with a jaunty bounce in her step. When she saw Amy, she stopped short, her mouth forming an "O" and her sparkling blue eyes stretched wide in surprise. "Miss Amy, did you come to fix my hair?"

Amy's mouth dropped open. She'd forgotten all about the promise she had made to the child. What in the world should she do? Sure, Hal had seemed to mellow out after her apology. But in light of their confrontation that afternoon, would he want Amy spending more time with his daughter?

Amy bent down, hands on knees, to tell the little girl that tonight might not be such a good time.

"Of course, she did," Hal said before the words formed on her lips.

Surprised, Amy glanced up. "You don't mind?"

"Number one rule of parenting, Miss Jordan. Never break a promise to a child."

Well, he really hadn't answered her question, but, at the moment, Amy didn't care if he minded or not. She was simply grateful she wasn't going to have to go back on her word to Krista.

Amy turned her attention back to the child. "Why don't you show me where you keep your brush and comb and we'll get started."

Stepping toward the door Krista had just come through, Hal mumbled something about cleaning up the kitchen.

A beaming Krista curled her hand around two of Amy's fingers and led her into a bedroom decorated for a little princess. A white canopy bed with a fluffy floral spread was complemented by a matching dresser with a vanity mirror, a chest of drawers, and desk. White Priscilla curtains added a touch of warmth to the pale pink walls.

But one area contrasted sharply with the rest of the room. Trucks, cars, brightly colored building blocks, balls and bats, all scratched and showing signs of frequent use, lined the shelves along one wall. Amy did notice three dolls perched high on the top shelf, looking abandoned. One of them hadn't even been taken out of her box.

Robert obviously hadn't been stretching the truth when he said Krista was a tomboy.

Amy noticed a framed picture of a woman sitting on Krista's nightstand. Curiously drawn to the photo, Amy picked it up and studied it. The woman, with dark curly hair and brilliant blue eyes, leaned against a tree, posing confidently for the camera. A seductive curve tipped the corners of her red painted lips. She was, Amy acknowledged, a rare beauty, possessing the kind of face one expected to find on the cover of a first-class fashion magazine.

"That's my mama," Krista said, answering the question roaming Amy's mind. "She died when I was little."

Amy smiled down at the little girl who looked so much like the woman in the photograph. "I know, and I'm very sorry." She returned the picture to the nightstand and scooped up the brush and comb from the dresser. She didn't want to dampen the child's high spirits by reminding her of her deceased parent. Amy knew from experience the heartache of growing up without a mother. Her own had died when Amy was only three.

She sat down on the bed, positioning Krista between her knees, and unwound the band from the child's ponytails. She was grateful Hal hadn't followed them. His absence allowed her to enjoy this time with his daughter without feeling under pressure from his judgmental parental eye. Amy was usually comfortable around people, new acquaintances included. But Hal Cooper's mere presence unnerved her in a way she couldn't define.

"Do you have any pets?" Amy asked as she pulled the

brush through Krista's thick curls.

"Yes. I have a dog. His name is 'Rufkin.' "

"Is he that beautiful golden Lab I met outside a while ago?"

"Uh-huh." Krista nodded. "And I have a guinea pig named 'Scooter.' "

"That must be that orange and white hairy thing over there in the cage in the corner?"

"Uh-huh." Krista bobbed her head up and down again, and Amy grinned, not bothering to remind the child she needed to be still while having her hair fixed.

"We can play with him when you get finished, if you want," Krista added.

"We'll see." Amy had never petted a guinea pig before, but the furry little creature darting around the cage, stopping occasionally to twitch his nose, appeared harmless enough. At least he didn't have a long tail like a mouse. Amy shuddered. She hated mice.

While she finished Krista's French braid, the child kept up an incessant chain of chatter. Amy was wrapping a band around the bottom of Krista's hair when Hal poked his head and one shoulder through the open doorway. "How's it going? You girls through primping yet?"

"Going great," Amy said. "We're just finishing up." She slipped the final loop around Krista's hair.

Krista abandoned Amy, running to her dad. In one smooth motion, he stepped through the door, bent, and lifted his child to his hip.

Amy stood back, watching the interaction between father and daughter.

"Am I pretty, Daddy?" Krista asked, turning her head and touching her braid.

The corners of Hal's eyes crinkled. "Yes, you sure are, Buttercup."

"Am I pretty as Miss Amy?"

Amy's heart tripped, although she couldn't fathom why. She knew how unpredictable kids could be. And she knew adults could be put on the spot in trying to answer a child's innocent yet awkward questions. She'd learned, during her short career, to take in stride any unorthodox thing that came "out of the mouths of babes." But, for some reason, she held her breath in anticipation of Hal's answer.

After only a second's hesitation, he said, "You're as pretty as the prettiest angel in heaven."

His wife, Amy immediately concluded. That's whom Hal was referring to. Though Amy knew little about the Bible, she had, over her years of sporadic church attendance, gleaned enough knowledge to know angels weren't human and humans weren't angels. But she could also see why Hal thought of his deceased wife as one. She was certainly lovely enough.

Figuring now was a good time to make her exit, Amy stepped forward. "I really should be going."

Hal looked back at his daughter. "Why don't you run and hop in the bathtub, and I'll walk Miss Amy to the door."

"Can Miss Amy give me a bath?"

"Now, Krista, how long have you been giving yourself a bath?"

Krista ducked her head. "Since I been four."

"We wouldn't want Miss Amy to think you're not a big girl, now, would we?"

Krista shook her head.

"Why don't you go thank her for fixing your hair, then go do as I asked. But leave the bathroom door cracked so I can hear you."

Hal set down his daughter. Artfully pouting, the child traipsed over to Amy.

Amy kneeled down, putting herself on the child's level. "You think I could get a hug?"

Krista reached up and wrapped her arms around Amy's neck. Amy returned the embrace, closing her eyes and relishing the feel of a child against her breast. These last few minutes with Krista had reminded Amy of how much she missed the time she'd spent with children while practicing medicine.

While Krista padded off to the bathroom, Hal followed Amy outside. Amy noticed he left the door open, apparently so he could listen for his daughter.

Stopping and looking up at him, Amy said, "Thank you."

He tucked his fingertips in his front pockets. "For what?"

"For allowing me to keep my word to your daughter. She's a lovely child. I enjoyed the time I spent with her."

"Thank you. I think she enjoyed herself, too."

"You're blessed to have her."

"Yes, I am."

An awkward silence passed between them, as though they were both unsure of what to say next.

Hal recovered first. "I'd walk you to your car, but. . ." He pointed a thumb over his shoulder.

Amy held up a palm. "Oh, no. I understand. You need to get back to you daughter."

Reaching for the doorknob, Hal nodded. "Good night, Miss Jordan."

"Good night." She started to walk away, but when she heard the door click shut behind her, she looked back and, like an obstinate child wanting to get in the last word, added, "Hal."

&

Amy didn't go home but returned to Robert's and Linda's for two reasons. Number one, she found the idea of facing four unpacked boxes so late in the evening depressing. Number two, her appetite had returned and her cupboards were still bare.

After eating her fill at her friends' table, she followed Linda to the living room where Robert sat back in a recliner with his face buried in a newspaper.

Adjusting a pillow along her side, Linda curled up on one end of the sofa. Amy slumped down on the other end, stretching out her legs and crossing them at the ankles. Lacing her hands over her stomach, she lay her head back, closed her eyes, and waited for the question she knew was coming. As expected, she didn't have to wait long.

"How did it go at Hal's?"

The inquiry, of course, came from the overly curious Linda, but Amy suspected Robert was indiscreetly directing an interested ear her way.

"I think your cousin hates me," Amy answered.

"Hate?" Linda's voice rose in surprise. "That's an awful strong word to use when referring to someone you know so little about."

Amy detected a note of defensiveness in her friend's voice, but wasn't surprised given Linda's fondness of Hal. Amy rolled her head to the side, opened her eyes, and met Linda's chiding expression. "Okay. 'Dislikes me' then."

The expectant mom crossed her arms. "Look, Amy, I know Hal lost his temper with you this afternoon, but that was because he's so defensive when it comes to Krista. He's not usually like that. I mean, he does have a temper when he's pushed too far, but he's not one to hold a grudge or hate someone because they ask a few questions about his daughter."

Amy shook her head. "I don't think it has anything to do with our discussion over Krista. In fact, he apologized for losing his temper with me."

"What, then, makes you think he dislikes you so much?"

Using her hands for leverage, Amy pushed herself up out of her slumping position. Folding one leg in front of her, she angled her body so she faced Linda. "For one thing, he insists on calling me"—she drew quotations marks in the air—" 'Miss Jordan.' For another. . ." Amy paused here, trying to find the right words to describe the resistance she sensed whenever she was around Hal. Finally figuring there was no clear way to explain something she didn't understand herself, she forged ahead. "For another, he seems to put up his guard around me, like he's wearing this iron shield of suspicion. It's as though he feels threatened by me in some way." She shrugged. "Only I can't fathom why."

Linda chewed on her thumbnail, studying Amy with intensity, then narrowed her eyes as though she were on the verge of figuring out some complicated math equation. "I think I know why."

Amy gave a helpless, palms-up gesture. "Then, please, tell me what great trespass I've committed to warrant his stand-offish attitude."

"You remind him of his wife."

Amy's eyebrows rose. "His wife?"

Linda nodded.

Amy scratched her forehead in confusion. "Ah, Linda, you're not making any sense. I saw a picture of Hal's deceased wife when I was at his house a while ago. I look nothing like her."

Linda adjusted her pillow. "No, you don't. She had dark curly hair, blue eyes, and probably stood at least a head shorter than you. But you do have one thing in common with her."

"What's that?"

"Beauty."

"Ha!" Amy's response rang with satirical disbelief. In her opinion, she was too tall and gangly. Maybe she had one or two good features to her benefit, but *never* had she thought herself beautiful. She certainly wouldn't put herself in the same class as a woman as lovely as Hal's deceased wife. "Linda, I think your pregnancy is doing weird things to your brain."

Tucking in one corner of her mouth, Linda shook her head. "Never mind. You don't get it. You never will."

An annoyed "Uh" left Amy's lips. "Linda, I do wish you'd stop talking in circles and explain what any of this has to do with Hal's attitude toward me."

"Adrienne, like you, was an extremely beautiful woman. She literally glittered when she walked into a room. Only she knew it, and took advantage of it."

Amy worried her right lower lip with her teeth. Was her friend saying what she thought? That the "angel" she saw in the picture at Hal's wasn't really an angel at all? "You mean, she used people?"

"Yes, she used people, including Hal." Pain surfaced in

Linda's eyes just before she averted her gaze downward. "Especially Hal."

Amy waited, wondering if Linda would explain what she meant by Adrienne using Hal. But she didn't, and Amy, although curious, didn't ask.

Amy wasn't quite sure what to make of this new revelation. Perhaps Hal hadn't been referring to his wife when he told Krista she was "as pretty as the prettiest angel in heaven." Guilt pricked Amy's conscience when she found a small degree of solace in that thought.

But she still couldn't see how she reminded Hal of his deceased wife, unless. . .

An alarming thought pierced her mind. She had grown up in a world where almost everybody used everybody else to get what they wanted. She had tried hard not to let herself fall into that self-serving mold, but maybe she hadn't tried hard enough. Her brow creased with concern. "Linda, I don't use people. . .do I?"

Linda rolled her eyes. "Of course you don't. That's exactly what I'm trying to say. All you have in common with Adrienne is your good looks, and, right now, that's all Hal can see."

Amy sent her friend a dubious look. "You mean, you think Hal somehow finds me attractive, and that turns him off?"

"Yep. My guess is he's trying to push you away because he's afraid of making the same mistake with you he made with Adrienne." She gave a nonchalant shrug. "But give him time. He'll eventually figure what really lies beneath your surface." An impish gleam lit up her dark brown eyes. "And when he does, it'll be interesting to see what happens between you two."

Amy recognized that look. Where her love life—or, rather, her lack of a love life—was concerned, her friend sometimes couldn't resist playing Cupid. "Don't go there, Linda. I didn't come to Cedar Creek looking for romance."

The warning didn't seem to phase Linda. Amy could already see the matchmaking wheels spinning in the brunette's head.

Amy made a pretense of examining her fingernails and, more for her own benefit than Linda's, added, "Besides, I get the feeling your cousin is a very complicated man. And the last thing I need in my life right now is another complication."

five

Hal eased his pickup to a stop in the driveway of Amy's new home and got out of the vehicle. He'd come to the rental house out of obligation, not desire. Most weeks, Sunday was his only day off, and he didn't want to miss an opportunity to spend a few quality hours with his daughter. But at church that morning, Linda had told him Amy was having trouble with the plumbing at the rental house. Since his mother was still out of town, he felt duty-bound to see if there was anything he could do to help out.

He climbed the steps and rang the doorbell. In a few seconds, a window curtain fluttered, then the door flew open.

Amy met him with a look of mild surprise. "Hal?" The inflection in her voice reflected the unasked question *What are you doing here?*

"Good afternoon, Miss Jordan." He tipped his head politely. "I saw Linda at church this morning, and she mentioned you were having trouble with the water."

Her shoulders drooped a bit. "I wish she hadn't told you that. I was going to wait until tomorrow before I called your mother. I didn't want to bother her. . .or you. . .on a Sunday."

"It's no bother." In the same breath, he asked, "What seems to be the problem?" He wanted to stay on track. The sooner he finished here, the sooner he could get back to Krista, who had conned him into letting her stay with Robert and Linda while he saw to his mother's new tenant.

"Well, the hot water runs but it doesn't get hot. And I just now tried the range top, and found it doesn't work, either." She gave a helpless palms-up gesture. "Am I doing something wrong?"

"Have you tried lighting the pilot lights?"

She blinked. "Pilot lights?" Sweeping a stray lock of honey-colored hair behind her ear, she added, "Excuse my ignorance, but I have no idea what a 'pilot light' is."

"Propane gas supplies the energy for the hot water, stove, and heat," he explained. "But to get those things to work, you'll need to light their pilot lights."

She looked at him like he'd just handed her an unassembled bicycle with no instructions on how to put it together.

He held on to his stoic expression despite the amusement threading through him. This girl was city through and through, just like Robert had been when he first moved to Cedar Creek. But from day one, Robert had put forth a dogged effort to fit in with the people of Cedar Creek. He'd determinedly learned their ways, accepted their lifestyle, and extended the first friendly hand.

It had taken some time, but, eventually, Robert's persistence paid off, and the usually reserved folks of the Cumberland Gap highland town had embraced the doctor as one of their own.

But what about this newcomer? Would she rise to the challenge like Robert had? Or would she find the old-fashioned and conventional world of Cedar Creek too inconvenient for her and run back to the city, like Adrienne had?

"Would it take you long to show me how to do that?"

Amy's question penetrated Hal's errant thoughts, which had strayed from amused to grim in a matter of seconds. He shook his head. "No. Not at all."

She stepped to the side and motioned him in, closing the door behind him. "Where do we begin?"

"How about the kitchen stove?"

She led him through the living room, where four cardboard boxes sat scattered about the floor, then continued on through the door leading to a modest dining room and on to the tiny kitchen located at the back of the house.

When she stopped in the center of the room, Hal walked past her to the pantry. "Mother always leaves a supply of matches in here on the top shelf." He opened the folding doors then froze, taken aback by the unexpected barrenness of the cupboard. He stared a blank moment at the empty shelves, then reached up for the matches. He withdrew a small cardboard box then closed the doors on the pantry— and on the disturbing wave of concern that had washed over him upon first viewing the stark shelves.

Amy was an adult. A grown woman, who, he was sure, could manage to find something to eat if she was hungry.

He turned away from the pantry and faced her. She stood next to the stove, her hands tucked in the back pockets of her jeans. When their eyes met, a timid smile touched her lips— and Hal thought he felt something thump him in the chest.

An uncanny sense of déjà vu swept over Hal, sending a wave of uneasiness up his spine. Why did she suddenly have such an arresting effect on him? There was absolutely nothing special in the way she wore her hair—pulled back in a pony-tail with that one stray lock trapped behind her ear. Neither was there anything deliberately provocative in what she wore—a simple white sleeveless blouse tucked into a pair of loose-fitting jeans.

Yet something twisted inside Hal. Something vague and abstract, yet all too familiar.

Reining in his emotions, he walked over to the stove and turned a knob. He would not let her innocent facade or her seemingly helpless state get to him.

He lit a match then touched it to the mouth of a tiny valve leading from one burner, explaining his actions as he went. A steady blue flame appeared.

Watching and listening intently, Amy leaned over his arm. Not close enough to touch him, but close enough that he felt the heat emanating from her body. And close enough that her pleasant, balmy scent slipped unbidden past the shaky control he held over his senses. He had to concentrate to remain focused on the task before him.

He turned the knob further, and a sapphire and orange circle of fire danced to life around the stove burner. "You see," he said, turning the control back and forth, making the blaze bigger then smaller. "You can adjust the flame, depending on how fast your food needs to cook."

"Neat," she said in awe. "Now I can cook over an open fire anytime I want, regardless of the weather."

A sting nipped at Hal's fingertips, and he remembered he was still holding the lighted match. He quickly blew it out.

He turned off the burner then strolled to the sink, where he turned on the faucet and held the blackened matchstick under running water. "Where's your trash can?" he asked, turning off the spigot.

"I haven't bought one yet. I went to the market this morning to buy a few supplies and some groceries." She shrugged. "I didn't realize it was closed on Sunday."

So that explained her empty pantry. Hal laid the matchstick in the sink, reminding himself once again that Amy's plight wasn't his problem. He was only there to light the pilot lights. "I'll show you how to light the water heater now. It's in the basement."

Hal led the way downstairs, but at the bottom remembered he'd left the box of matches on the kitchen counter. "Wait right here," he told her, turning back, "I forgot the matches."

He trotted back up the stairs and was reaching for the matchbox when a piercing scream rent the air. Panic ripped through his chest. "Amy?" He abandoned the matches and ran for the stairs.

She met him at the top, flying into his arms and wrapping her own around his neck. He teetered back a couple of steps, struggling to maintain his balance. "Amy, what's wrong?"

She jumped and squirmed and latched onto him like a python squeezing the life out of its victim. "Get it, Hal! Get it! Get it!" she screamed in his ear. "Don't let it come up here!"

"Amy, what are you talking about?" He tried to loosen the grip she had on his neck, but she merely tightened her hold. Burying her face in the crook of his neck, she mumbled something unintelligible.

Hal somehow managed to slip one arm beneath her gyrating knees and lift her twisting body up into the cradle of his arms. The second her feet left the floor, she stopped squirming. But she didn't loosen her ironclad grip on him, and she kept her face hidden against his neck.

He lumbered to the living room and lowered her to the sofa. When he tried once more to pull her arms from around his neck, she only squeezed harder. Hal had no choice but to ease down and sit on the edge of the sofa next to her.

"Amy, sweetheart," he said, cajoling her with the same firm but gentle voice he sometimes used on Krista, "you're choking me. You're going to have to let go."

Her arms relaxed a bit, but she still didn't release him. So he let his hands rest on her waist and waited. Soon, her labored breathing steadied, and her arms slackened a little more.

"There you go." He slid his palms up her sides to her upper arms. Finally, she allowed him, albeit reluctantly, to draw back enough so he could see her face. She released his neck, letting her hands fall to her lap.

The look of fear in her green eyes hit him full force. His chest contracted. The errant lock of hair had worked free from her ear and now curled along her jaw line. Reaching up, he tucked the wayward strand back behind her ear. Then he cupped the side of her face with his palm and brushed her cheek with his thumb. "Now, tell me what happened."

"I saw a m–mouse."

Hal's caressing thumb went still. "A mouse?" He couldn't believe it. All this excitement over a harmless little rodent?

She nodded. "Yes. Oh, Hal." She shook her hands like she'd stuck her fingers in something slimy. "It was big and hairy and had a long tail. And its eyes. . ." Tears pooled on her lower lids. "Oh, Hal, it looked at me."

Hal wrapped his arms around her and pulled her close, trapping her fluttering hands between them. He rocked her back and forth, holding her head against his shoulder, trying to console her. But at the same time, he fought hard not to laugh. He'd seen the reaction of people who were afraid of mice before—he'd danced around one or two himself. But never had he witnessed such a desperate response as Amy's. It almost made him pity the mouse, which was probably huddled in some dark hole right now still trying to recover from Amy's earth-shattering scream.

"It's okay, now," he said when he finally regained control of his mirth. "The mouse is downstairs. You're up here."

"Will it stay down there? I mean, can it get up here?" Her voice sounded so small. So. . .*defenseless.*

Hal became acutely aware of her long lashes fanning his neck every time she blinked. A peculiar flutter rose in the pit of his stomach. His remaining mirth fled.

Slowly, he stopped rocking as an intense stillness settled over the room. The kind of heart-stopping, motionless silence that preceded a first kiss.

Amy drew in a shaky breath and released it with a shudder. The warm air slipped inside his collar and whispered against his chest, tugging at a forbidden place there, a door he'd long ago locked and vowed to never reopen again. Gooseflesh pricked the back of his neck.

He closed his eyes, battling temptation. He wanted to kiss her. Tip her chin and taste the sweetness of her lips. Quench the thirst parching the back of his throat.

But he wouldn't. Not this time. He'd fallen for a beautiful woman once, but never again. He was eight years older and a hundred years wiser now. Clinging to his last thread of resistance, he captured her upper arms and backed away.

Amy gazed up at him with misty green eyes full of an emotion he did not want to define. Unshed teardrops glistened on her tawny lashes. He resisted the urge to reach out and wipe the moisture away.

"Tell you what I'll do," he said. "I'll go to my house and get some mousetraps and put them out. I'll set two on the top step. There's not a mouse alive that can resist a baited trap."

Her eyes searched his with skepticism. "Are you sure?"

Hal smiled. "I'm sure." Although, he really wasn't. But going after the traps would at least get him out of her presence long enough for him to cool off.

"Okay," she finally replied, her voice still weak and trembling. She leaned back, pulling her knees to her chest and wrapping her arms around them.

Hal rose. "I'll be back in a few minutes."

Amy nodded, but her gaze roamed the floor like she expected a beady-eyed rodent to dash across the room at any given second.

Hal made his way outside and to his pickup, drawing in a deep, settling breath of pine-laced mountain air. Thank God, he'd made his escape.

As he reached for the truck's door handle, he heard the front door of the house open and close. Looking up, he found Amy dashing down the porch steps, slipping her narrow purse strap over her shoulder.

"Wait up," she said. "I'm coming with you."

෴

Hal set the second baited trap in the corner of the top basement step. "There you go." Standing, he glanced over at Amy, who stood with her back hugging the opposite wall. "Do you want me to show you how to light the pilot light on the water heater now?"

Her gaze darted past him to the darkened stairway tunnel; then she looked back at him like he was daft. "You mean, go back down there?"

"Never mind," he said, wondering why he'd even bothered asking the question. "I'll do it." He held up a paper bag containing four more traps and some cheese. "I'll set these out while I'm down there."

"Okay," she readily agreed.

Flipping on the light, Hal loped down the stairs. Before he reached the bottom, he heard the door at the top close. Shaking his head, he couldn't help grinning.

When he came back up, he found Amy pacing the living

room floor, her arms folded across her midsection. She stopped and faced him as he entered.

"You should have hot water in a couple of hours," he told her.

"Did you set the other traps?"

A smile tugged at his mouth. Apparently, hot water had slipped down a notch on her list of priorities. "Yes." He tucked his thumbs into the back pocket of his jeans. "Try not to get too close to them, though. They're quite easily sprung and painful if you get a finger caught in one," he added, although he felt quite certain he didn't need to worry about her getting close enough to one to trip it.

"What do I do if I catch a mouse?"

"Dispose of the body," he said, just to see her reaction.

"What!"

Guilt pricked his conscience at the sight of her wide-eyed terror. "Call me, and I'll take care of it."

Her entire body relaxed.

Raising her right hand, she ran her fingertips across her forehead, focusing on some unknown spot below his chin. "It must seem silly, me being so afraid of a mouse. But, I can't help it." She dropped her hand and met his gaze. "Some people are afraid of heights, some closed-in spaces. My phobia is mice."

"Don't worry about it. I understand." Hal was afraid of horses—almost as much as Amy was of mice. But he decided he'd keep that bit of information to himself.

He glanced at the boxes scattered about the room. "I see you haven't finished unpacking."

"Finished? I haven't even started, yet."

Frowning, he looked back at her. "Is this all you have?" The words slipped out ahead of his thoughts. Too late, he realized the question was a personal one.

Dropping her gaze back to the unknown spot below his chin, she shifted her weight from one foot to the other, and Hal sensed his thoughtless inquiry made her uncomfortable.

"Well, sure," she said. "My apartment in Atlanta was furnished." Once more lifting her eyes to his, she smiled, but it seemed forced. "You don't know how grateful I am that this house is, too."

Hal studied the woman in front of him, Linda's words from the evening before coming back to him. *"Would you please try and make Amy feel welcome? Life hasn't been so good to her lately, and she could use another good friend right now."*

What had Linda meant? Hal could only guess.

Amy Jordan possessed class and sophistication, grace and beauty. That much he knew. But what else did she own?

Her personal belongings were contained in four cardboard boxes sitting in the middle of the living room floor of a rented house. Her food pantry was empty, and she drove a fourteen-year-old car. Granted, that car was a convertible and in mint condition, but it was an older car just the same. Perhaps a remnant from better days?

Like a wave cresting in the ocean, a desire to pull her into his arms, tell her everything would be all right, that he'd be her friend and take care of her swept over Hal.

But his common sensibilities rose to do battle with his tumultuous emotions and won. He'd be a fool to think allowing himself to become personally involved with Amy would stop at friendship. She was too alluring, too tempting.

Too beautiful.

All he felt for her was physical attraction and pity. He didn't know her well enough for the churning in his stomach, the pounding of his heart, and the sweat on his palms to be anything else. And he knew too well where surface attraction and sympathy for a seemingly defenseless woman could lead if he wasn't careful.

He decided he'd done his duty to his mother's tenant. He'd seen she had a stove top to cook on, hot water, and set some mouse traps. He'd worry about lighting the furnace later, when the weather, and he, had cooled off a bit.

"Well, I guess I should go pick up Krista. Robert and Linda are watching her for me and are probably ready to pull their hair out by now."

Amy followed him to the door, which he opened without hesitation. When he stepped outside, her soft-spoken "Hal?" stopped him. He turned around to face her.

She leaned in the doorway. "Thank you for lighting the pilot lights and setting out the mouse traps. I apologize for disrupting your Sunday afternoon."

He gave her a curt nod. "No problem. Have a good afternoon, Amy."

She smiled, her eyes sparkling like a kid's on Christmas. "I see you remembered my name."

Hal hadn't meant to call her by her first name earlier. It'd just slipped out when she screamed, and when she was hanging onto him for dear life—when his guard was down. Now, he feared going back to the more formal 'Miss Jordan' would sound a little ridiculous, making his efforts to keep her at arm's length too obvious. "If you prefer, I can—"

"Please, no!" She grimaced, holding up a protesting hand. "I hate being called 'Miss Jordan.' It makes me feel too old." She hunched one shoulder. "Besides, we're neighbors. I'm your mother's tenant. There's no reason we can't be on a first name basis, is there?"

"No," he had to begrudgingly agree. "I suppose there isn't."

"Good." She pushed away from the door frame and reached for the doorknob. "I'll see you later."

He started to walk away, but a rumbling sound stopped him in his tracks. He glanced at Amy's midsection, where the noise had come from.

She folded her hands over her stomach. "Excuse me. All that excitement a while ago has kicked up my appetite."

He met her gaze. An embarrassed blush was rising in her cheeks.

"Amy, how long has it been since you've eaten?"

She frowned thoughtfully, like she was trying to remember. "Last night. I went back to Robert's and Linda's after I left your house."

That did it. Knowing she was hungry coupled with her

having no food in the house ripped away the defenses he was barely managing to hold intact.

He captured her wrist, pulling her across the threshold and closing the door behind her.

"What are you doing?" she wanted to know.

"Taking you to get something to eat." He led her to the steps.

She resisted. "Like this?"

He stopped and looked at her. "What do you mean, like this?"

"I'm a mess. I need a bath."

She was a mess all right. The prettiest mess he'd ever laid eyes on. "You won't have any hot water for at least another hour and a half," he reminded her.

Her gaze darted to the front door, then back to him, like she was torn between making herself presentable and satisfying her hunger.

As though rallying for her attention, her stomach growled again. She released a relenting sigh. "At least let me get my purse."

Why women insisted on carrying around extra baggage had always been a mystery to Hal. But he knew better than to argue with a woman over her handbag.

He released her wrist. "Okay. I'll wait right here."

When she disappeared into the house, he drew in a deep, replenishing breath. He could do this. He could take her to his house, fix her a meal, fill a bag with enough food for a couple of days, and bring her back here without allowing himself to fall under her spell.

But first, he'd go pick up Krista. Having his daughter around to provide a buffer between him and Cinderella Jordan would definitely help.

And it did.

While Hal cooked Amy a man-size hamburger and a generous serving of French fried potatoes, Krista kept Amy occupied in the living room building a log cabin—with the same set of wooden logs he'd played with as a child. Then, during the meal, his daughter sat at the table and chatted with Amy while he packed two bags with food from his own pantry.

Two hours later, still unscathed by the fierce attraction he felt for her while in her presence, he delivered her back to the rental house.

Or so he'd thought.

But later that evening, as he sat in his easy chair, his Bible open to a still-unread passage of scripture, images of the green-eyed beauty pushed everything else from his mind.

He thought of the way her hair, a honey-hued mixture of white, gold, and brown strands, caught the light when she tilted her head a certain way. The way her eyes, as bright and green as new leaves in spring, captured and held his gaze at an unexpected moment. The way she smelled, like a dew-kissed field of clover, when he held her close that afternoon. The feel of her warm breath against his neck. . .

Those memories of her, he feared, would linger deep in his conscious for a very long time.

But he had other memories. Shattered fragments from his life with Adrienne he gathered up now to remind him where his attraction to Amy could lead if he wasn't careful.

"I'm doing good, ain't I, Daddy?"

Krista's young voice penetrated Hal's reflective reverie. He shifted his gaze from the obscure spot he'd been staring at on the opposite wall to his daughter. She sat cross-legged in the middle of the living room floor, finishing the miniature log cabin she and Amy had started earlier that afternoon. He didn't bother correcting her grammar. In Cedar Creek, "ain't" was an accepted part of the everyday vocabulary.

Krista peered up at him, her blue eyes wide in anticipation of his answer. Her dark curls were once again secured in a neat French braid, compliments of Amy.

Odd, he thought, Krista had never really cared how she wore her hair before. Of course, he probably couldn't have done anything about it if she had. He still found getting her pigtails straight a challenge.

"Yes, Buttercup," he said in answer to her question. "You are doing good."

"Wanna help me finish?"

"Sure."

He rose, sauntered over to his daughter, and lowered himself to the floor. He had more important things to focus on than his attraction to Amy Jordan. The most important of all was sitting right here in front of him.

He picked up a log and showed Krista how to start building the roof. He'd done his neighborly duty this afternoon by lighting the pilot lights, setting the mouse traps, and seeing that Amy had food through tomorrow. But given his reaction to the newcomer, he'd be wise to avoid any close encounters with her in the future.

In the past, he'd had always looked after the minor repairs on his mother's rental house. But, while Amy lived there, he'd simply hire someone to take care of whatever problems arose.

Yep, he thought with determination as he placed another log on top of the cabin. The safest path he could take was the one leading away from Amy Jordan.

six

"Well, here it is." Robert said as he pushed open the door of Amy's new office.

Amy stepped forward, scanning the modest room. A computer sat on a simple oak desk, a built-in supply cabinet lined the wall on one side of the room, and a long credenza stood beneath a single window along the back wall. A hand-carved coat rack was nestled in one corner, a tall ficus tree in another.

Simple and unobtrusive, Amy thought. Exactly what she needed. A place where she could fade into the woodwork. No excessive demands. . . No parents wanting her to wave a magic wand and instantly make their child well. . . No eminent expectations. . . Just a steady nine-to-five job she could leave at the office at the end of the day.

"I know it's not what you're used to," Robert added, stepping up next to her.

"It's perfect, Robert."

"I figured that's what you would say. You never did care much for glitz and glitter. It was always the people. That's what made you such a good doctor."

Amy felt Robert's gaze on her but refused to look at him—and she chose to ignore his last comment. She didn't want any reminders of what had been. Walking down the hallway a short while ago had been hard enough. Each examination room she passed brought back a bittersweet memory.

Shaking off the melancholy spirit threatening to dampen her enthusiasm for her new job, she strolled to the desk and brushed her fingertips across the smooth desktop, then thumbed through the stack of invoices resting in a letter tray. She opened a top desk drawer and found an assortment of gem clips, ink pens, and notepads all neatly organized inside.

Overcome with gratitude, Amy shook her head. Robert and Linda had done everything possible to make Amy's transition to this new world an easy one. They would have probably had her pantry stocked with food had she not insisted she was going to take care of buying groceries the day she arrived in town. But after her distressing tryst with Hal that first evening, the last thing on her mind had been grocery shopping.

A smile touched Amy's lips as she thought of the time she spent with Hal yesterday. He had been cool and aloof when he'd first come to check on her hot water problems, but, before long, his gentle nature had shown through. He was, Amy suspected, a generous and caring man. A softy at heart.

He was also the most virile man Amy had ever met in her life. Whenever she was in his presence, everything and everyone else just seemed to fade into the background.

Then there was his daughter. The little girl had managed to worm her way into Amy's heart the first time Amy had laid eyes on the child.

A dreamy sigh left Amy's lips as she sank down in her chair. Hal and Krista Cooper. Now, there was a pair a woman could easily fall in love with—if that woman were in a position to fall in love.

"What's that smile about?"

Robert's voice shattered Amy's daydream, jerking her back into the real world. She looked up to find him standing in front of her desk, his arms folded across his chest, grinning at her like he knew her innermost thoughts and found them amusing.

"I, um, was just thinking how fortunate I am to have you and Linda as friends. You've made this move so easy for me."

As though summoned by the mention of her name, the spunky, expectant mom poked her head inside the open door. "Robert, Ann Peters is on the phone. She said the cream you prescribed for Casey doesn't seem to be helping his rash."

"Okay," Robert said, turning toward the door. "I'll talk to her."

When the couple disappeared around the doorway, Amy breathed a sigh of relief. Somehow, she had to stop thinking so much about Hal. He had been on her mind almost constantly since Saturday night.

Rolling up to her desk, Amy reached for the invoices in the letter tray and went to work. Although Linda or Robert hadn't had a chance to show Amy anything about how to operate her new terminal, she plunged right in, completely undaunted by her lack of computer skills. After all, how hard could posting a few accounts payable be?

By midmorning, she'd found out. The computer kept telling her she was performing an illegal operation. About the sixth time the ornery machine told her she was breaking the law, she wanted to toss the thing out the window. She thought an illegal operation was something performed by a shady doctor, not a novice office manager trying to work her way through a stubborn software program.

She left work at the end of that day with a new respect for the office staff she had, in the past, taken for granted. By the end of the week, she was beginning to fear she had made a mistake in trying to tackle her new position.

But she gave herself a dozen pep talks over the weekend, then approached week number two with a new determination. By the end of her tenth day at work, things had settled down to a dull roar. But Amy's initial enthusiasm for her new job was fading fast.

Even though she was feeling more comfortable and confident with the position, the daily tasks didn't offer her the excitement and challenge practicing medicine had. But, she reminded herself often, it did fill her days. And to occupy the long, lonely evening hours, she took up a new hobby—house painting.

❧

"You lied, Joe."

Paint roller in hand, Amy stood in the center of the extra bedroom of her new home, studying the wall she had, with her landlady's permission, started painting. A drop cloth covered the carpeted floor. A paint can, paint brush, and a half-full paint tray sat at her feet.

Joe, a nice, friendly man at the hardware store, had helped her choose the supplies she needed for the project. When she had checked out, he'd smiled, winked, and told her, "You'll do fine, ma'am. They ain't nothin' to paintin' a bedroom."

Well, she begged to differ with Winking Joe. She had more paint on her T-shirt and jeans—which she'd worn only twice before—than she had on the wall.

With a disparaging shake of her head, she bent down to moisten her roller, but a smile of deliverance touched her lips when the phone rang. Leaving the roller in the paint tray, she abandoned her task and raced to the living room, answering on the third ring. "Hello."

"Hey, Amy. This is Robert."

"Hi, Robert. What's going on?"

"I'm at the clinic."

Amy frowned. It was Saturday evening. What was Robert doing at the clinic—unless he had an emergency?

"What's wrong?" As the question left her lips, a picture of Robert's pregnant wife flitted through Amy's mind. When Amy had spoken with Linda earlier that day, the expectant mom hadn't been feeling well. Amy's pulse accelerated. "Is Linda okay?"

"Linda's fine. But. . .Amy. . ."

Something in the way Robert said her name sent a chill of apprehension down her spine. After a long, tense pause, he added, "I need your opinion on something."

Amy's grip on the phone tightened at the same time a lump of dread rose in her throat. "What?"

"A patient's blood work."

Bingo! Amy had feared Robert would eventually try to involve her with his patients, try to convince her to return to practicing medicine. Her only surprise was that he'd waited two weeks to make his first move.

"Robert, you know just as much about analyzing blood counts as I do." She heard a defensive ring in her voice, but couldn't help it. Robert needed to realize her decision to quit practicing had been final.

"Not in this case, Amy. This is a child. And, quite frankly, I have no idea what I'm dealing with here."

Amy found that hard to believe. Robert graduated medical school in the top three percent of his class. He certainly wasn't lacking knowledge when it came to analyzing blood samples.

Mentally, she put up a shield of resistance. Robert had always had a knack for talking her into doing things she didn't want to do. But not this time. She would stand her ground. Her emotional survival depended on it. "Call a specialist if you have a question," she suggested.

"I could, but. . ."

Robert paused again, and Amy tapped an agitated foot while she examined the white paint freckles on her hand. She would not let Robert's persuasive plea get to her. *She would not.*

"Amy, it's Krista."

Amy's petulant world stopped spinning so abruptly the room tilted. The specks on her hand blurred and the *tap, tap, tap* of her foot fell silent. "Krista?" she repeated in a small voice.

"Yes."

A picture of the little girl flooded Amy's mind. Her sparkling blue eyes, her cherubic smile—the ugly bruises on her arms. Amy's eyelids slid shut. Krista really was sick after all.

"Amy? Are you still there?"

"Yes." Opening her eyes, she swallowed. "Robert, I don't know if I can—"

"Please, Amy. Krista looks like someone has beaten her black and blue. Both she and Hal are really scared right now, and, to be honest with you, so am I."

Amy raked a lock of hair away from her face and squeezed her eyes shut. For the love of Pete, what should she do?

"Amy?"

Robert's voice sounded urgent, and small, like a lost little boy wandering the aisles of a huge department store in search of a parent.

She swallowed hard, fighting the fingers of fear closing around her throat. "Okay. I'll be there in a few minutes."

"Thanks." Amy heard relief in Robert's sigh.

She hung up the phone and retrieved her purse from the bedroom. As she climbed in her car, the thought crossed her mind that she was about to see Hal. She was even less presentable now than she had been the last time she'd seen him—when he showed up on her doorstep two weeks ago to tackle her hot water problems. But, there was no time for vanity now. A child was sick and needed her.

She started to whisper a prayer but stopped herself short of uttering the first word. The last time she'd asked God for help, a little girl had died. Either He had chosen to ignore her plea, or He didn't exist at all. She cranked her car, shifted into reverse, and backed out of the driveway. Either way, she didn't see much point in wasting her breath on prayer now.

❧

Krista sat on Hal's lap, her head resting against his chest, his arms wrapped loosely around her. Although he wanted to hold her tighter, he was afraid to. It seemed everywhere he touched her, she'd bruise right before their very eyes.

"Daddy, I want to go home now."

Her small, scared voice echoed exactly what Hal felt. He raised a hand and ran his palm down her dark curls. "I know, sweetheart. Uncle Robert will be back in a minute, then, maybe we can go home."

Hal checked his watch then glanced at the door. What was taking Robert so long, anyway? When he'd pricked Krista's finger and drawn blood, he'd said he'd have the results in less than five minutes. That had been twenty minutes ago.

Hal's fear increased with each passing second. Something was terribly wrong. He knew it. Why else would Robert be gone so long?

A few minutes later, Hal could stand it no longer. But at the same time he decided to go in search of Robert, the door opened and the doctor walked into the room. Hal searched his friend's face. Robert was smiling, but the two undeniable lines of strain creasing his forehead didn't go unnoticed by Hal.

"Well?" Hal asked, both anxious and afraid to hear what Robert was about to say.

Although moving at his normal pace, Robert seemed to take an eternity to pull his stool from beneath a built-in desk and sit down. Then, he took the time to take off his glasses, fold them, and tuck them into his shirt pocket. For the first time in the two years he'd known the doctor, Hal wanted to choke the man.

Folding his arms over his chest, Robert finally spoke. "Hal, Krista's platelet count is low."

Hal swallowed, but the fist of fear refused to dislodge from his throat. Somehow, he managed to speak around it. "What, exactly, does that mean?"

"To be perfectly honest with you, I don't know."

"You don't know?" Hal's voice rose in uncontrollable ire on the last word.

"No. But I've called in another doctor. A pediatrician who may be able to shed some light on what might be going on with Krista."

Hal took a moment to rein in his frenzied emotions. "Okay. When will he be here?"

"*She* is already here, and, with your permission, I'd like her to come in, do an examination on Krista, then speak with you about Krista's blood workup."

Hal was totally baffled. Where had Robert found a pediatrician in Cedar Creek this fast, at this time of night? But, those questions would have to be answered later. All Hal wanted right now was for someone to tell him his daughter was going to be all right. He nodded his consent. "Sure. Send her in."

Robert rose and opened the door, peeking around the corner and motioning for the mystery doctor to enter. Amy Jordan, the enchantress who had haunted Hal's dreams the past two weeks, appeared and stepped into the room.

Shock sent his caustic nerves reeling. He looked from one solemn face to the other, then his brow dipped in befuddlement. "Robert, what's going on here?"

"Hal, Amy is a licensed pediatrician," Robert explained. "She practiced in Atlanta before coming to Cedar Creek."

A pediatrician, my eye, thought Hal. *If Amy Jordan was a doctor, what was she doing working as an office manager?* Instinctively, his arms tightened around his daughter, and he turned away slightly.

"Hal, Amy is a good doctor," Robert added, apparently noticing Hal's protective gesture. "In fact, she's the best pediatrician I know."

Hal didn't know what to do. He knew he could trust Robert, but what did he know about Amy? Not much, he quickly concluded.

As though reading his thoughts, Amy raised a hand and ran her fingertips across her forehead. "Look, Robert, I don't want to do anything that makes Hal uncomfortable. I'll call the specialist in Lexington and see how soon he can see Krista." With that, Amy turned and strode out of the room.

Hal leveled Robert with a dark scowl. "Robert, what's going on here?" he demanded for the second time.

The doctor looked at the door thoughtfully, as though he could still see the woman who had just walked through it. "Hal, you've just met the real Amy Jordan." Then he looked back at Hal. "I think she can help Krista, if you're willing to let her."

☙

Amy was seated at her desk about to dial the phone when Robert walked into her office. "Amy, wait." He closed the door and stepped closer. "Hal's changed his mind."

Amy returned the receiver to its cradle. "Robert, I don't think this is such a good idea."

"Hal was just surprised to learn you're a doctor. That's all."

"Duh." Amy leaned back in her chair and gave an "I wonder why?" palms-up gesture. Then, she leaned forward on her folded forearms. "I'm *not* a doctor anymore," she reminded her friend. "All I agreed to do was come in and give you my opinion on Krista's blood work." Shaking her head in disbelief, she added, "I don't know why I let you talk me into examining her."

"Because you care."

Amy dropped her gaze to her desktop to escape Robert's knowing expression. She did care, she begrudgingly admitted to herself. More than she wanted to.

Robert released a despondent sigh and Amy looked up to find him rubbing his closed eyes with his thumb and forefinger. He looked tired. And worried. And Amy knew he had reason to be.

"Amy," he said, dropping his hand, "I'm dealing with a monster here I've never run across before."

"I'm not one hundred percent sure I have, either, Robert," Amy answered, repeating what she'd told him in the lab room earlier while studying Krista's blood sample through a microscope. "Further testing needs to be done by a pediatric hematologist. Krista is going to have to see a specialist anyway."

"I know. But the closest one is in Lexington, which is two hours away, and that's if we can get Krista in to see him tonight. Can you imagine how long the next few hours are going to feel like to Hal if he doesn't have a clue as to what's going on with his daughter? Couldn't you at least go in there and give him something to hang on to until he gets Krista to Lexington?" Robert braced his hands on Amy's desk. He searched her face a moment with intense brown eyes, as though trying to find a part of her that was missing. "Then, it'll be out of your hands," he finally added, "and you can walk away. . .if you want to."

That's exactly what Amy wanted to do—what she intended to do. She leaned forward on her elbows, closing her eyes and circling her temples with her fingertips. Tears pushed at the back of her eyelids, but she refused to let them escape. In spite of the heaviness bearing down on her chest and the tightness in her throat, she voiced her biggest fear. "What if I'm wrong, Robert? What if Krista is sicker than I suspect?"

"Then, at least you'll know you tried."

Amy squeezed her eyes shut tighter. She didn't want to do this. She didn't want to walk back into that examination room and face her old demons. But the mental picture of Krista sitting on her daddy's lap, looking all bruised and battered, and Hal, looking like he'd lay down his own life for a tiny thread of hope, became larger than her own fear. And, somewhere deep inside her, she found a remnant of strength and knew she could make it through the examination. Somehow, some way, she'd make it. Then, she'd go home, break down, and start putting the past behind her all over again.

Opening her eyes, Amy met Robert's hopeful expression. "Okay, Robert," she said. "I will tell Hal what I suspect. But, I'm only doing this as a friend. Not as a doctor."

His entire body slumped with relief. "Thank you."

Walking down the hallway alongside Robert, Amy drew in a deep breath of courage. Why was she doing this? *How* could she be doing this? What was propelling her forward? One short month ago, thoughts of walking into an examination room again as a doctor sent her emotions spiraling out of control, like a penny in a wishing well. And each time she found herself, like that copper coin, at rock bottom.

The answer almost knocked Amy's wobbling legs out from under her. Hal and Krista. She was doing this for a charming lumberjack and his sparkling-eyed little girl. The realization touched on something inside Amy she never knew existed, a door that had never before been opened. She wasn't sure what it was, or that she even wanted to open that door and explore what was beyond it. She just knew her legs quit shaking and her steps grew faster—and stronger.

Then a voice Amy had never heard before rose from somewhere deep within and told her that for the sake of Hal and Krista Cooper, she could do just about anything.

seven

When Amy and Robert reentered the examination room, Hal gave Amy a quick head-to-toe perusal. He still had a hard time believing she was a doctor. She certainly didn't look like his perception of the high-class pediatrician Robert had described a few minutes ago. Her hair was pulled back in a ponytail—except for that one wayward lock that insisted on curling along the soft curve of her right jaw. She'd twisted the ponytail and fastened it at the crown of her head with a gold barrette, leaving the end of her long golden strands fanning her head like a peacock's tail in full spread. She wore a green T-shirt, light denim jeans, and pale blue canvas shoes, all of which appeared relatively new, but they were speckled and smeared with something that looked like white paint.

But in spite of her less than professional appearance, Robert had assured Hal she was a *good* doctor. No, not just a good doctor—the best pediatrician he knew. And given the current dilemma Hal faced, he had little choice but to entrust his daughter into the care of this woman he knew so little about.

May as well start off on a good note, he thought. "Look, about the way I reacted a while ago, I—"

"It's okay," she said with a wave of her hand, cutting off his weak attempt at an apology. "I understand."

Hal nodded, relieved she didn't appear offended.

Without looking at Robert, Amy held out her hand. At the same time, he unhooked his stethoscope from around his neck and handed it to her, as though he'd read her mind as her thoughts unfolded. Hal was surprised when a spark of jealousy shot through him.

Hooking the ear pieces of the stethoscope around her neck, Amy strolled across the room, knelt beside Hal, and lay her hand on Krista's back. The child responded by burying her face in the front of her daddy's shirt.

Dread rose in Hal's stomach. Krista hated coming to the doctor, and he had a feeling she was about to show one unsuspecting pediatrician just how stubborn she could be.

"Krista, honey," Amy coaxed, "have you ever listened to your heartbeat?"

Krista turned her head and peered at Amy, who held up the cupped end of the instrument. After a few thoughtful seconds, Krista shook her head.

"Would you like to?"

To Hal's amazement, Krista nodded, pushed away from his chest, and reached for Amy. Reluctantly, he released his daughter to the doctor, who gently carried the child to the examination table and set her down.

Amy fit the ear pieces of the stethoscope into Krista's ears, then held the cupped end to Krista's small chest. After waiting a few seconds, Amy asked, "Do you hear that?"

Krista nodded.

"That's your heart."

A brilliant smile accompanied by an expression of awe spread across Krista's face.

Amy waited another moment, then said, "May I listen now?"

Krista's head bobbed up and down.

While Amy fastened the ear pieces into her own ears, Krista asked, "Are you a real doctor, Miss Amy?"

Amy paused, looking at Krista as though the question had caught her off guard, then smiled. "Tonight I am." She lifted the instrument to his daughter's chest.

"Just for tonight?" Krista wanted to know.

With the forefinger of her free hand, Amy touched Krista's nose. "Just for you."

In a matter of seconds, the examination was well under way. Hal stood close by watching in amazement as Amy teased and cajoled his young daughter, who only a few short minutes ago had been just as scared as he, into full cooperation. Before long, Krista was so entranced by Amy, Hal had a feeling the child had forgotten all about his and Robert's presence.

Mentally, Hal shook his head, thinking back to two weeks ago, when he'd witnessed Amy's panicked reaction to a mouse. Could this really be the same woman he thought so helpless and vulnerable?

Upon finishing the examination, Amy helped Krista slip her shirt back on. "Do you like to draw?"

"Uh-huh."

"Good." Amy lifted Krista off the table, but instead of handing her back to Hal, passed her to Robert. "Let's see," Amy said, looking around. "You'll need some paper." She snapped her fingers, like she'd just received a bright idea, then circled around to the foot of the examination table and slipped the large roll of white paper off the end. She held the paper out to Robert, whose mouth dropped open in surprise. "Relax," Amy told him, "I'll order an extra roll next week."

Robert snapped his mouth shut and gave a consenting, one-shouldered shrug. "Whatever you say, Doc."

"Now for some pens." Amy rummaged around in a drawer until she found a red and a green felt pen, then she plucked Hal's pen from his shirt pocket, and Robert's from behind his ear and held them all out to Krista. "Here's red, green, blue, and black. I want you to go with Uncle Robert to my office and draw me a pretty picture for my wall."

Face brightening, Krista reached for the pens. "Will you really put it up?"

"Of course. You can help me pick out a frame, and we'll hang it together."

"Promise?"

"Promise."

Krista left a happy camper, and Hal found his own spirits a little lighter at seeing his daughter's jovial mood. But when Amy turned and faced him with a serious expression, he sensed the worst was yet to come, and his brief moment of ease dissipated like steam in a cold wind.

She motioned for him to sit. Then she rolled the doctor's stool directly in front of him and eased down onto its bright yellow cushion. Crossing her long legs, she grasped the sides of the seat and leaned forward slightly. "Do you know anything about platelets, Hal?"

"Just that they have something to do with clotting the blood."

"That's exactly what they do. A normal platelet count is between one hundred forty thousand and four hundred thousand." A short pause, then, "Krista's is fifteen thousand."

Hal's eyebrows shot up and his head jutted forward. "Fifteen thousand!" He did some quick calculating in his head. "That's only about ten percent of what she should have."

Amy nodded. "That's why she's bruising so easily right now. She doesn't have enough platelets in her blood stream to clot her blood properly, so she's bleeding underneath the skin."

Hal wanted to scream—to stand up and ram his hand through the wall. Why was this happening to his daughter? Struggling to keep a cap on his tumultuous emotions, he swallowed the fist of fear threatening to choke him. "Can you tell me what's wrong with my little girl?"

"I think so." She shifted, uncrossing then recrossing her legs in the opposite direction. "Has Krista had a viral infection over the past few days? Something you wouldn't normally bring her to the doctor for, like an upset stomach or a cold?"

"Well, yeah. She had an upset stomach and ran a low-grade fever a couple of days ago." Guilt stabbed at Hal's conscience. Should he have brought Krista in sooner? "She was better the next day, though, so I figured she just had a twenty-four hour bug."

Amy smiled as though that bit of information pleased her. "I'm sure she did."

"Does Krista having a stomach virus have something to do with her low platelet count?"

"I think it has everything to do with it."

He shook his head. "I don't understand."

"I think Krista has a rare blood disorder known as Idiopathic Thrombocytopenia Purpura."

He pulled a face. "Idiowhat?"

"I know." Amy rolled her eyes as though the long, complicated name frustrated her as much as it did him. "Let's just call it 'ITP' for short." She shrugged. "Besides, by the time you learn to say it, I'm counting on Krista being better."

Hal saw a ray of hope and grabbed it. "You mean there's a cure?"

"No, there's no cure—"

His shoulders drooped.

Amy held up a protesting hand. "Now wait a minute. Hear me out."

Hal nodded.

"With ITP, when a child gets a virus, for some reason yet unknown to the vast array of researchers in the medical field," she made a wide sweep with her arm, "her antibodies attack her platelets, destroying them faster than her bone marrow can reproduce them. Now, while there is no cure, there is treatment."

"There is?" He leaned forward slightly.

"Yes. In fact, there are several, the most recent drug is given through an IV over a twenty-minute period."

"Can you do that here?"

"I'm afraid not, at least not in the beginning. Krista needs to be under the care of a pediatric hematologist, and the closest one is in Lexington. Also, just to be on the safe side, the doctor there will probably want to do a bone marrow test to make sure nothing else is going on with Krista. And since this is her first known bout with low platelets, I suspect he'll want her to stay in the hospital for a few days, at least until her platelet count returns to a safe level."

"So, what you're saying is, this can happen over and over again, right?"

"It's possible. For a little while, anyway. But, remember what I told you. I'm counting on Krista being better by the time you learn to say the," she drew quotation marks in the air,

" 'ITP' word." She dropped a warm hand to his knee. "Hal, I know the cloud hanging over your head right now looks pretty dark, but, I assure you, there are some silver linings, and I want you to keep those in mind." With her free hand, she ticked off the silver linings. "Number one, this is not a terminal illness; number two, its not communicable—she can't pass it on to anyone else; and number three, 90 percent of the children with ITP completely recover within one year."

He considered what she said and had to agree, things could be a lot worse. At least his daughter had a 90 percent chance of recovering. "What about the 10 percent that doesn't recover?"

The optimism in her eyes faded a bit. "If Krista happens to be among the 10 percent that doesn't recover, then you deal with it. While she will have bouts with low platelets, and during those times you'll see the inside of a doctor's office so much you'll be tempted to take her and run the other way, remember there is treatment. But the majority of the time her platelet count will most likely be normal, and, with a few precautions, she should be able to lead a full, productive life."

He nodded. "I'll try to remember that. In the meantime, I'll pray for her healing."

Amy dropped her gaze and pulled her hand away from his knee. "I'm going to go make the call to Lexington," she said. "My feelings are they'll want you to take her in tonight. I'll have Robert bring her in so you can prepare her."

"Okay. Thanks."

He thought she was going to get up then, but, instead, she reached over and slipped her long, slender fingers around his hand resting on his thigh. Squeezing his hand, she said, "I really think Krista is going to be fine, Hal."

Their eyes met, and Hal felt the warmth of her gaze slip past his defenses. He curled his fingers around hers, drawing strength from her touch, and studied the sincerity in her expression. For the first time since meeting her three weeks ago, he allowed himself to catch a glimpse of the gentle, caring person emerging from behind her exquisite beauty, and, he had to admit, he was beginning to like what he saw.

🍃

Amy breezed back into the room after making the call. "All set. They'll be waiting for you as soon as you can get her there."

Hal stood beside the examination table, where Krista sat finishing her picture. "Great," he said, reaching for his daughter. "I'll leave from here." He propped Krista on his hip.

Amy's heart twisted. The poor man appeared ready to do whatever he could as fast as he could to help his daughter.

"Do you have anyone to go with you?" Robert asked.

Hal shook his head. "No. Mom left early this morning. It's her weekend to sit with Aunt Lucille. I'll call from the car and let her know what's going on. She'll probably want to get one of her sisters to swap out so she can come to the hospital. Krista and I will be fine until she gets there, though."

"It's a two-hour drive to Lexington, Hal, and Krista may need your attention during the drive," Robert reasoned. "Let me make a quick call to Linda, and I'll ride up with you." Turning to Amy, he said, "You don't mind staying close by in case Linda needs you for anything, do you?"

"Of course not."

"Thanks. I'll be right back." He headed for the door.

"Wait," Amy stopped him. When he turned back, she said, "I know Linda wasn't feeling well this morning, and I'm sure you don't want to leave her. Why don't I go with Hal and Krista?"

"You don't mind?"

She shook her head. "No. Not at all."

Robert shifted his gaze to Hal. "Is that okay with you?"

Amy's stomach knotted then. What was she doing? She had vowed to remain uninvolved, to walk away after the examination. Glancing at Hal, she held her breath. Maybe he'd say he had someone else who could ride with him, then she'd be off the hook.

"Sure," he answered to her dismay. Turning to her, he added, "In fact, I'd appreciate it. . .very much."

Amy forced a smile. So much for walking away.

eight

As Amy expected, the pediatric hematologist at Lexington diagnosed Krista with ITP and recommended she be treated just as Amy had described to Hal. Once in the bloodstream, the medication would attract the attention of the antibodies that were attacking her platelets and give the blood-clotting cells a chance to rebuild to a normal level.

Amy had witnessed countless children being hooked up to IVs and, each time, had managed to remain emotionally detached. But not this time. Hearing Krista cry when the nurse injected her tiny hand almost broke Amy's heart.

Fortunately, Krista's pain was short-lived, and now, two hours later, Amy stood just inside the door of Krista's hospital room watching Hal while he watched his sleeping daughter. His mother, Ellen, stood on the opposite side of the bed.

This wasn't the first time Amy had witnessed a family pulling together in a crisis, but it was the closest she'd ever come to being a part of that experience. After her own mother died, it had been the nanny who'd bandaged her boo-boos, driven her to the doctor when she was sick, sat beside her hospital bed when she was eight and had to have her tonsils removed. Her father had been there before the surgery, but he hadn't been there when she had awakened in the recovery room. He had merely telephoned from time to time, whenever his surgery schedule allowed.

Whenever there wasn't a crisis in Amy's life, he usually didn't check in at all.

A nurse coming in to check Krista's vital signs interrupted Amy's somber ruminations. Amy shook off the melancholy spirit threatening to overshadow her. But she couldn't shake off the fatigue and weariness invading her body—that all-too-familiar feeling that had been her constant companion the weeks immediately following her breakdown.

Suddenly, her surroundings closed in on her. Visions of another hospital, another room, another little girl rose up to haunt her. A smothering weight bore down upon her chest.

She needed to get out. Out of this room, out of this building, out into the night air where she could look up at the sky and see the stars and remind herself that another world existed. A world that didn't include hospital rounds, late nights at the office, an endless list of patients. . .dying children. A world where she now belonged. Somehow, she had to find her place in it.

She retrieved her purse from the chair where she had dropped it earlier and eased the thin strap over her shoulder. Just before slipping out the door she glanced back at the people, the family, she was leaving behind. Her gaze lingered on Hal. He leaned over and lightly brushed his daughter's forehead with his lips.

A lump caught in Amy's throat. It was the most beautiful sight she'd ever seen.

ॐ

Gazing down at his daughter, Hal shook his head in awe. "It's amazing how she can sleep so well after all that excitement a while ago." The child lay in peaceful slumber, as though the trauma she had experienced two hours before had been two years earlier and long forgotten.

Ellen Cooper reached over and swept a curl away from her granddaughter's cheek. "Children are resilient that way."

"Yeah. That's what Amy said on the way up here," Hal replied without looking up.

A half-smile tugged at the corner of his mouth as he recalled that moment. They had been en route to the hospital, and Amy was behind the steering wheel of his SUV, leaving him available to Krista should she need him. After Krista had fallen asleep in the backseat, he'd told Amy he was worried about how Krista would handle the tests and treatments when she got to the hospital. Amy had reached over, squeezed his hand, and said, "It'll be rough at first, but once treatment is over, she'll settle down pretty fast. Children are resilient that way. They usually handle things a lot better than grown-ups do."

Pulling his thoughts back to the present, Hal, not for the first time, silently thanked God for Amy's presence. She had a way of knowing what to say to calm his fears whenever they started getting the best of him. It was as though she had some sort of internal sensor his nervous system activated whenever he was on the verge of panic.

"Speaking of Amy, where did she go?"

Hal glanced up at his mother, who was looking past him with a befuddled frown creasing her forehead. He turned toward the door, where Amy had been standing a few short minutes ago, only to find her gone. He slid his gaze to the chair where she had earlier dropped her purse and discovered it missing also.

He left his daughter's bedside and ambled to the door, looking both ways when he stepped out into the hallway. Midnight had come and gone over an hour ago. The dimly lit corridor was empty except for two nurses busy with paperwork at the nurses' station. Hal traipsed down the hallway and checked with the nurses. One had seen Amy leaving, but neither knew where she had gone.

Puzzled, Hal turned and walked away. Where could she have gone, and why hadn't she told him or his mother she was leaving?

Stepping back into the room, he said, "I think I'll walk around a bit, see if I can find her."

"Oh, Hal, give the poor girl a few minutes to herself." The slim, agile grandmother left her granddaughter's bedside and plopped down in a nearby chair. "She's probably just gone to freshen up a bit, scrape off some paint she didn't have a chance to get rid of before coming up here. I'm sure she'll be back in a minute." Brushing a strand of short, silver-streaked hair away from her face, she laid her head back and closed her eyes.

Hal stood there, considering his mother's theory, and figured it was more logical than anything he could come up with.

Ellen cracked open one eye and patted the seat beside her. "Why don't you come over here and rest while Krista's sleeping? You never know when she may wake up and need you."

Hal lumbered to the chair and sat down, but found his gaze slipping to the door every few seconds.

Less than two minutes later, his mother, without opening her eyes, said, "Don't worry about Amy, Hal. She's a big girl. She can take care of herself."

Hal didn't know how to respond. After thirty-two years, his mother's perceptiveness still sometimes amazed him.

He settled down in the chair. He knew his mother was right. Amy was a big girl; she could take care of herself.

Still, something about not knowing where she was made him uneasy, raised his protective instincts. Knowing she had the keys to his car in her purse didn't help any, either. But, surely she wouldn't leave the hospital alone in the middle of the night. . .would she? That last thought subtly reminded Hal of how little he knew about Amy Jordan.

He stretched out his legs, crossed them at the ankles, and clasped his hands over his abdomen. One hour. He'd wait one hour; then he'd go look for her. After another vigilant glance at the door, he laid back his head and closed his eyes.

Four imperceptible hours later, he opened them.

He sat up, massaging the kinks out of the back of his neck. Blinking the sleep from his eyes, he checked his watch. Five-thirty A.M. Man, he hadn't meant to fall asleep, much less check out for four hours.

He looked up at the hospital bed, and found his daughter still resting peacefully, then glanced over at the only chair in the room that had been unoccupied when he drifted off, expecting to find Amy curled up there. But the chair was empty. A quick glance around the room told him she had either returned and left again, or she hadn't come back at all. Something akin to panic rose in his chest.

His mother stirred, rubbing her eyes as she sat up. "Krista apparently rested well. How about you two?"

"Amy's not back yet," Hal said, carefully guarding the tone in his voice against his rising anxiety. He did not want to alarm his mother. "I'm going to look for her," he added, standing. "If Krista wakes up, tell her I'll be right back."

Eyes widening with concern, Ellen nodded, and Hal strode from the room in search of Amy.

His search ended a few minutes later when he found her in the pediatric waiting area, sound asleep.

Smiling, he stepped into the room. She made quite a fetching picture lying there curled up on the sofa, one flattened hand serving as her pillow, her purse held securely against her chest. The light from the lamp on the end table above her head reflected off her hair like sunshine on a field of ripened wheat.

Then Hal's steps slowed. She looked different than when he'd last seen her. Instead of a twisted ponytail, she now wore her hair in her characteristic neat French braid. She'd also replaced her paint-spattered T-shirt, jeans, and tennis shoes with a pale yellow blouse, a full-length light green skirt with a pale yellow floral pattern, and brown sandals. His smile faded and his brow dipped in a disconcerting frown. Where had she gotten the change of clothes. . .? He searched his brain for an answer and soon came up with the only possible one. She *had* left the hospital. . .in the middle of the night. . .*alone*.

He clenched his teeth, a swift surge of anger shooting through him. Didn't she know what kind of crazy perverts roamed the city streets at night?

๛

Something awakened Amy. Not a sound, or a touch, but a sense she was not alone. She opened her eyes to find Hal standing in the middle of the room, gazing down at her with the oddest expression on his face. His scowl reminded her of the time she had fallen running away from the snake out on Bear Slide Hollow and knocked herself out. She had awakened then to find him frowning down at her pretty much the same way he was now.

Amy's stomach fluttered. Hal Cooper, with his full day's growth of beard shadowing his wedge-shaped jaw and cleft chin and his finger-combed short hair, was not a bad dream to wake up to.

Sitting up, she sent him a sleepy smile. "Good morning." She shielded a yawn behind one hand. "What time is it?"

"Five-thirty," he answered without looking at his watch, then he strode over and sat down beside her. Leaning forward, he propped his elbows on his knees and let his hands dangle between them. Instead of looking at her, he stared straight ahead in pensive silence, like he had a heavy thought on his mind.

"Is Krista okay?" Amy asked, hoping his somber mood didn't mean otherwise. Everything had appeared fine when Amy returned to the hospital a little over an hour ago. She'd peeked in the room and found him, his mother, and his daughter all sound asleep.

"She's fine," he answered to Amy's relief. "Still sleeping."

"That's good. How about you and your mom? Did you get much sleep?"

"A little."

Amy chewed her right lower lip, considering the firm set of his bearded jaw and his clipped answers to her questions. "Is something wrong, Hal?" she finally asked.

He turned his stoic expression on her. "Amy, where have you been?"

"Oh." She looked down at her new outfit, only then remembering her middle-of-the-night shopping spree. Raising her head, she met him with a pleased smile. "Shopping."

His eyebrows inched upward. "Shopping," he repeated in an *Are you serious?* tone.

"Yes." Amy bent forward, reached way back beneath the sofa, and came up with a large plastic shopping bag. "I found a variety store that was open all night and bought us all a change of clothes." She reached into the bag. "I hope everything fits. I had to guess at the sizes."

"Amy, what on earth were you thinking?"

She detected a note of ire in his voice and stopped short of pulling out a pair of jeans. Looking up, she found his expression belligerent. She frowned in befuddlement. "I was thinking if we all wore the same clothes the entire time Krista's in the hospital, we wouldn't find much pleasure in each others' company," she told him.

"Don't you realize how dangerous it is for a woman to be out roaming the city streets at night alone?"

His condescending tone sparked her indignation. It had been a long time since anyone had reprimanded her for anything she did—*a very long time.* She leveled him with a *Just who do you think you are?* glare and said, "I suppose it's a lot less dangerous for a man to be out roaming the city streets at night."

"That's not the point."

"Oh?" She lifted a cynical brow. "Then what is the point?"

Clearly frustrated, he ran a hand down his face.

"Are you upset because I drove your car?" she asked, then before he could answer added, "Because, if you are, I can assure you I brought it back without a scratch and with a full tank of gas."

His brown eyes turned two shades darker. He clenched his teeth. "You mean you stopped at a service station?"

She refused to flinch under his mounting wrath. "Yes."

"And got out of the car?"

"Yes."

"And pumped gas."

"Yes."

He shook his head, looking at her like she'd just lost her last marble.

She gave him a palms-up gesture. "I don't understand what you're so upset about."

"I'm upset because. . ." He hesitated, his mouth hanging open as though whatever he meant to say had gotten lodged

in his throat. After a brief, paralytic moment, his features softened and his shoulders drooped. In a much gentler, much
softer voice, he said, "I was worried about you."

In his now-tender eyes, she saw how much that admission
had cost him, like he'd let go of some sacred part of himself.

Her anger fled and any further argument died on her
tongue. For years she had traveled the streets of Atlanta at all
hours of the night, going to and from school, work, and the
hospital, and no one had ever worried about her safety before.
A warm glow settled deep within her chest.

"It's probably because I'm from such a small town," Hal
injected, like he'd jumped back on his treadmill of thought
after temporarily slipping off. "You know how it is." He gave
a nonchalant shrug. "We're pretty snoopy people, us mountain folk. We know every time our neighbors go out their back
door, we watch each others' houses during vacations, we
always tell someone when we're leaving. . ." His voice trailed
off like he'd just run out of bumbling excuses.

Amy grinned.

"What?"

"Stop apologizing, Hal, before you convince me you really
didn't mean it."

Aiming a thumb toward the bag, he said, "What'd you get
me?"

A quick change of direction, she noticed. Pulling out a pair
of jeans, she said, "Jeans, relaxed fit. Hope you can wear
thirty-three thirty-threes."

One corner of his mouth tipped. "That's exactly what I wear."

"Good."

She also showed him the plaid cotton shirt she'd bought
him, pink overalls for Krista, and khaki slacks and a peach
blouse for his mother. She left the toiletries and bare essen-
tials in the bottom of the bag. She didn't have the nerve to ask
him what size underwear he wore.

"I don't have enough cash on me to reimburse you for the
clothes right now," he said while she stuffed the clothes back

into the bag, "but I'll pay you back when we get home."

"That's okay. You don't have to."

"Of course, I do," he said, sounding a little offended.

Men and their pride, she thought. "Whatever," she said, figuring arguing with him was pointless.

He nodded, apparently satisfied with her answer.

Amy slipped her hand through the hand-holes at the top of the bag. "Let's go see if Krista's awake."

He reached over and took the bag from her—another gentlemanly gesture she wasn't accustomed to. "Okay, but. . ."

She cocked a brow. "But?"

He playfully bumped her shoulder with his. "Next time you get the urge to run off in the middle of the night, let me know, and I'll go with you."

Amy's moonstruck heart wanted to believe he was talking about forever, but her rational mind told her he was only referring to their stay at the hospital. Reminding herself that now was not the time in her life to engage in foolish romantic notions, she sent him a mock salute. "Aye, aye, sir."

He rewarded her with a heart-stopping grin. "Come on," he said, pulling her up as he stood. "Let's go see my daughter."

He dropped her hand before they took the first step. Amy tried to convince herself the letdown feeling spearing her heart wasn't disappointment.

As they walked down the hallway, Amy couldn't help breathing an inward sigh of relief that he hadn't asked her the big question: Why had she left her practice?

While she realized she had gotten through one conversation without having to answer the question, she also knew that, eventually, he would ask. And when he did, she'd have to tell him. After all, she'd examined Krista. As her father, he had a right to know.

Then, he'd probably never let her touch his daughter again.

≈

"Amy?"

Hal and Amy stopped and turned to see who had called her

name. A tall, sandy-haired man with a stethoscope draped around his neck stood in the middle of the dimly lit hospital corridor, a look of utter disbelief on his face.

"Brandon?" Amy said, her voice ringing with surprise.

"Well, I'll be," the man responded. He stepped forward, his arms wide open. "It *is* you."

Amy left Hal's side and floated, it seemed, into the man's embrace.

The hug was. . .friendly. Too friendly for Hal's liking.

An unpleasant memory flashed through Hal's mind. He mentally pushed it away, reminding himself this was a different woman, different circumstances. He had no claim on Amy, no right to feel such intense jealously at seeing her in another man's arms.

When Amy and the man she'd called "Brandon" released each other, the stranger kept her close by holding onto her upper arms. "Girl," he said. "I was afraid I'd seen the last of you when I left Atlanta."

"I hate to disappoint you," Amy told him, "but here I am."

"The last thing you could ever do by showing up unexpectedly is disappoint me."

Hal noticed the way the man looked at Amy, like he couldn't get enough of the sight of her. And Amy smiled up at him like she'd found a long-lost treasure.

I should leave, Hal thought. Slip away so Amy and her old acquaintance could reminisce. Better that than what he *wanted* to do—step forward and physically remove the other man's hands from her arms.

"Are you on staff here?" Brandon asked, hope evident in his question.

Amy's expression changed. Both the sparkle in her eyes and the smile on her lips faded. "No," she said, the delight in her voice gone. "I'm here with friends." She stepped back, breaking contact, and turned to Hal, bidding him forward.

As Hal approached them, he read the name tag attached to the man's shirt pocket. "Dr. Brandon L. Copeland. Midland

Pediatrics." So, he was a pediatrician. Was he merely an old colleague of Amy's? Or more? Hal tried to ignore the unsettling wave of disquietude the thought brought to his stomach.

Amy slipped her hand into the crook of Hal's arm and introduced him to the doctor. The two men shook hands.

"Hal's daughter is here, she's being treated for ITP," Amy explained.

"Oh, man, I am so sorry," Brandon told Hal. "How is she doing?"

"She had a good night. We won't know if her platelets have gone up, though, until after blood counts are done later this morning."

"I hope she does well."

"Thank you."

Turning his attention back to Amy, the doctor said, "I ran into Dr. Cape at a convention a couple of weeks ago. He told me you'd left Mercy."

Hal felt Amy's hold on his arm tighten. "Yes. I did."

"Where are you practicing now?"

Her gaze dropped to the doctor's neck or his tie or some point well below his face. "Actually, I'm not practicing anywhere."

Brandon's jaw dropped in an incredulous gape. "What?"

Amy said nothing.

Now would be the proper time to leave, Hal thought. But Amy's hold on his arm kept him glued to the spot. It was as though she clung to him for support.

"Amy," Brandon said, inching forward, his expression full of concern. "What happened?"

"It's a long story, Brandon. I really don't have time to get into it right now. We need to get back and check on Krista."

"Sure. Maybe we can all get together for lunch while you're here."

Brandon glanced at Hal, and Hal nodded his approval. But Amy said a more negative, "We'll see."

The doctor studied Amy another bewildered moment, his

face etched with a dozen unasked questions, then he turned back to Hal. "I'll keep your daughter in my prayers."

Hal nodded. "Thank you, Doctor. I appreciate that."

Brandon reached over and squeezed Amy's hand, giving her one more worried look, then turned and walked away.

With a forlorn expression, Amy watched the doctor retreat. What was she thinking? What was she feeling?

"Life hasn't been so good to her lately." For about the hundredth time over the past two weeks, Hal recalled Linda's words about Amy.

What happened, Amy? he wanted to ask. *What made you leave such a successful career and come to work as a clinical office manager in a town where people still, at times, bartered to pay their medical bills?*

She'd traded so much for so little. Why?

The question would have to remain unanswered for now. If she didn't want to talk about it to an old friend like Brandon, then she wouldn't want to talk about it to Hal, whom she'd known hardly a month. And as much as he wanted to, he had no right to ask.

In silence, Amy turned and continued toward Krista's room. Hal followed suit, wishing he could do or say something to wipe the sad look off her face.

If he only knew what put it there.

&

Later that afternoon, Amy began to wonder if she should remain at the hospital for Krista's entire stay. It wasn't like she didn't have a way home; both Hal's and his mother's vehicles were at the hospital. There was nothing to prevent her from taking one of them and going back to Cedar Creek.

What would Hal and Ellen want her to do? If they wanted her to go, would they say so? Or would they, out of politeness and propriety, put up with her unwanted presence?

Amy chose a moment when she and Hal were in the vending room getting soft drinks to find out.

She leaned with one shoulder against one cola machine

while he fed coins into another. "You know, Hal, if you want me to, I can take your mother's car and go home."

He stopped short of pushing the selection button and looked at her like he didn't quite know how to respond to her statement.

"Or I can stay," she added, hunching the shoulder not leaning against the machine. "It's up to you."

"What do you want to do?" he asked, his finger still poised over the button.

"Whatever I need to do. I mean, I don't want to get in the way. On the other hand, if there's anything I can do here to help out, I don't mind staying."

He pressed the button. The machine groaned, then spat out the can. Leaning forward, he retrieved the drink, the entire time remaining quiet and pensive. Was he stalling, trying to figure out how to tell her to go home without sounding like he really wanted her to?

Straightening, he finally said, "What about the clinic? Can Robert do without you there for a few days?"

"Yes. I'm sure he'll understand, and I'll have plenty of time to catch up when I get back."

"Then stay." He paused long enough to pop the top on the can. "Krista may need you."

Krista may need me, but what about you, Hal?

The instant the question popped into Amy's head, she mentally shoved it away. She wasn't sure she would want to know the answer.

nine

On Wednesday morning, after three days with a steadily climbing platelet count, Krista was released from the hospital. But paperwork, at-home instructions, and a delay in the arrival of the required departure wheelchair prevented the Coopers and Amy from leaving Lexington before early afternoon.

Upon arriving back in Cedar Creek, the first stop was the Cooper house where Krista, tired from the busy morning and the long ride home, fell promptly asleep. Hal tucked Krista into her bed, then, with his mother there to watch over his daughter, he drove Amy home.

Somewhere between his house and hers, a melancholy spirit fell over Amy. While she was thrilled at Krista's speedy recovery, she was also saddened her time with the Cooper family was coming to an end.

For the past three days, Hal, Ellen, and Krista had treated Amy like a veritable member of their family. They'd included her in their decisions, their worries, and their concerns. Shared with her their laughter. No doubt, Amy would miss their companionship.

She cast a sidelong glance at Hal. She'd miss being with him most of all. A comfortable camaraderie had developed between her and the handsome lumberjack during Krista's hospital stay. What would happen to their budding friendship now that they were returning to their separate lives?

As Hal turned into her driveway, imminent loneliness welled up inside Amy. In a few short minutes, she'd be right back where she'd always been. Alone.

Hal eased his SUV to a stop and switched off the engine. "Well, here we are."

" 'There's no place like home,' " Amy quipped, forcing

100

counterfeit cheerfulness into her voice. "Thanks for the ride, Hal." Without hesitation, she reached for the door handle. *No point in putting off the inevitable.*

"Wait a minute. I'll get that." Hal was out the driver's seat and circling the front of the vehicle before she could protest.

Ever the gentleman, he held onto her hand while she stepped out of the four-by-four. His touch spawned a giddy flutter in the pit of her stomach. That same peculiar sensation had visited her often over the past three days—every time Hal was close enough for her to inhale his pleasant outdoor scent or feel the heat emanating from his body. Like he was now.

He dropped her hand and, side by side, they ambled up the walkway. The sun cast long, dreary shadows across the yard. A slight nip in the air and nearby shade trees touched by gold and brown hinted that fall was just around the corner.

Autumn, Amy thought as she climbed the front porch steps, *a time of year when the earth's bounty died, wasted away like sand filtering through a bottomless hourglass.*

Digging in her purse for her key, she thought of spring, hoping to dispel the somber mood she'd slipped into. Her efforts did little good. No matter how many images of March flowers and daylilies she summoned to mind, at that particular moment, the season of rebirth and new beginnings seemed too far away, a place in time she simply couldn't reach.

Hal took the key from her, unlocked, and opened the door. As he passed the key back to her, she turned to face him. "Maybe I'll see you and Krista in a couple of days, when you bring her to the clinic to have her platelets rechecked." She cringed inwardly. She'd failed miserably at trying to keep the "wishful thinking" tone out of her voice.

He hooked his thumbs in his hip pockets. "I wanted to talk to you about that."

"Oh?"

He nodded once, but said nothing.

After a few bewildered seconds, Amy figured out he was waiting for her to ask him in. "Would you like something to

•

drink? Coffee or tea?" she asked.

"Coffee sounds good."

Stepping across the threshold, she tipped her head sideways, silently welcoming him inside.

❧

"Can I do anything to help?" Hal asked, following Amy into the living room.

"No. Just make yourself comfortable, and I'll be back in a few minutes." With that, she disappeared through the door leading into the kitchen.

Hal sank down onto the sofa, taking in his surroundings as he did so. Nothing much had changed since the last time he'd been there. The cardboard boxes were gone. A decorative white ceramic jar and a half-burned green candle in a brass holder had been added to the mantle. A green and white afghan was neatly draped over a rocking chair sitting next to the fireplace. But he didn't find a single family photo, memento, or anything that appeared to have any sentimental value. Nothing that would give him a glimpse into her past, except the white Bible with gold lettering lying on the coffee table.

He leaned forward and read the inscription on the bottom right corner of the book. "Amelia Nicole Jordan." The name beheld a classical, yet mysterious presence. Much like the woman herself.

Reaching over, he picked up the Bible, testing the feel of it between his hands. He loved God's word. It and its Author had seen him through the most trying times of his life.

He opened the book and found a note written to Amy in a bold, familiar handwriting inside the front cover.

> *To Amy on her sixteenth birthday.*
> *Welcome to the family of God.*
>
> > *Your Friend Forever,*
> > *Robert*

A thread of envy wove through Hal. Robert knew Amy so

well, knew things about her he himself was only beginning to catch a glimpse of. Her likes and dislikes. Her pet peeves and common idiosyncrasies. . . Had Robert's relationship with her ever gone beyond friendship?

Hal shook off the unsettling thought. Even if it had, it was in the past. Robert was now happily married to Linda, and they were expecting their first child. And Linda seemed just as devoted to Amy's friendship as Robert.

Hal read Robert's note to Amy again. It appeared Amy had become a Christian shortly before her sixteenth birthday. Something akin to hope sprang up inside Hal. If she shared his faith, then maybe. . .

Before the entire thought could evolve, Hal pushed it away. It took more than one hand to count the reasons a relationship between him and Amy wouldn't work. She was everything he wasn't—elegant, cultured, highly educated. She was a doctor. She'd probably been to school twice as long as his twelve years. Then, there was the money—the evil root that had destroyed his marriage.

During Krista's hospital stay, Hal had learned Amy was not only a doctor, but also a doctor's daughter. Physicians from cities like Atlanta made big bucks compared to a sawmill operator from the Cumberland Gap Mountains. Amy had most likely grown up surrounded by wealth and luxury. Although, glancing around her sparsely decorated living room, one would never guess her affluent background. If she had money, why did she choose to live so simply?

Hal shook his head, mentally putting a halt to the confusing questions crowding his mind. If he wasn't careful, he'd start inventing reasons why a relationship between him and Amy might work.

He closed the Bible and set it back on the coffee table, reminding himself why he was there—to see if Amy would agree to be his daughter's pediatrician. Not explore ideas of starting a romantic relationship with her.

Hal had just leaned back on the sofa when Amy reentered

the living room carrying a mug in one hand and a large foam cup in the other.

"Straight up, no cream or sugar," she said, handing him the mug. "Sorry about the caffeine, though. All I have is decaf."

He smiled. She'd learned he liked his coffee strong and black and loaded with caffeine during their stay at the hospital. "Decaf's fine. Thanks."

Amy sat down in the recliner flanking his side of the sofa, kicked off her sandals, and curled her legs beneath her. Holding up her foam cup, she said, "I couldn't find any cups when Linda and I went to the flea market last week. Thank goodness, Frank sells these in his grocery store."

"I don't mind drinking out of the foam cup," he told her.

She grinned. "I'd trade, but I've already poisoned mine with cream and sugar."

"In that case, I guess the mug will have to do." He raised his drink in a mock salute, then took his first sip of coffee. The thick, ceramic container he drank from, he knew, was a free giveaway for opening a new account at the local bank. He'd received one just like it last week when he'd opened a savings account for Krista.

He watched over the rim as Amy gingerly drank from the large gaudy cup that looked totally out of place in the circle of her slim, delicate hands. She was a woman meant to hold fine china.

What happened, Amy? Why are you here? Why did you leave Atlanta?

The questions remained unanswered. Since her encounter with Dr. Copeland Sunday morning, she hadn't mentioned her practice, and she deftly dodged questions about her past. Sometimes Hal wondered if she'd evolved from thin air, a figment of his imagination too good to be true.

After her second dainty sip, she lowered the cup to her lap. "What was it you wanted to know about Krista's appointment on Friday?"

Raking aside his plaguing thoughts, he balanced his mug

on one thigh. "I was hoping I could convince you to see Krista through her illness. At least until we know she's completely recovered from the ITP."

Some indefinable emotion flickered in her eyes. "In what way?" she asked, her voice underlined with caution.

"She needs a pediatrician."

"She already has a good doctor."

Sensing resistance, Hal shifted in his seat. This was going to be harder than he thought. But his daughter needed a pediatrician, and Amy was the top candidate, so he plowed ahead. "You're right. Robert is a good doctor. One of the best, as far as I'm concerned. But the hematologist in Lexington said Krista needs to be under pediatric care between her visits to his office, and Robert's not a pediatrician. He said himself he has no experience with ITP."

Amy lowered her lashes, focusing on the milky liquid in her cup. Her rebellious lock of hair slipped free from her French braid and curled along her jaw. "I can't do what you're asking, Hal," she softly said. "I no longer practice medicine."

Why? The question circled his mind like horses on a runaway carousel. Should he press for an answer?

He wasn't sure if it was his growing need to know more about her or a selfish desire to satisfy his own curiosity, or both. But something urged him forward. He slid to the edge of the sofa, setting his mug on the timeworn coffee table. Bracing his elbows on his knees and clasping his hands between them, he willed her to look at him. When she did, he chose his words carefully.

"Amy, you diagnosed Krista's blood disorder when Robert couldn't. I've watched you interact with my daughter for more than three days. You're obviously a very gifted doctor."

"So, why did I quit?" she said, supplying the question he so desperately wanted answered.

He nodded.

A sad smile touched her lips. "I've been wondering when we would get around to this conversation."

"I don't mean to pry. If you don't want to talk about it, I understand."

She shook her head. "You're not prying, Hal. You need to know."

"I do?"

"Yes, you do. You're Krista's father, and since I examined her, you need to know why I no longer practice medicine. Then you'll understand why I can't take over as her doctor."

His interest acutely piqued, he settled back in his seat.

She lowered her gaze to her cup once more, tracing the rim with one fingertip. "It happened almost four months ago. I had just finished with my last patient and was about to start some paperwork when a nurse brought me a file. . . ."

Hal listened intently while Amy told him about a little girl named Jessica Jones, the critical error that led to the child's mistaken identity, and the little girl's untimely death. While she spoke, her voice remained steady, almost a monotone, like she was intentionally keeping her emotions detached from her words.

After she finished, Hal sat in silence, considering what she'd said. Was she telling him she'd left her practice because she lost a patient? For some reason, Hal didn't think so.

Doctors lost patients. That was an unfortunate fact of life that went with their vocational territory. Robert had lost a young woman to leukemia last year. Hal remembered the haunted look the doctor had worn for several days after that. But Robert didn't give up. On the contrary, he got up each morning and went to the clinic more determined than ever to serve the patients that remained.

What had been the difference for Amy?

Now that he thought about it, she didn't seem like the type, either, who would walk away from a career she obviously loved and had spent years preparing for because of a patient's death—tragic as that death was. Hal had spent enough time with her over the past three days to know she was levelheaded, strong, and intelligent—too smart not to have considered the repercussions of losing a patient before ever entering into the field of pediatrics.

A sixth sense told him something was still missing, a small kernel of understanding he hadn't grasped.

Driven by his need to know more, he leaned forward again, planting his elbows on his knees. "What happened after Jessica died, Amy?"

Her head came up. "I went back to work." Then, as though she couldn't bear facing him, she glanced away, but not before he caught a reflection of shame in her eyes. "I know that sounds hypocritical, Hal, being in the profession of saving lives when you're responsible for the loss of one."

So that was it. She blamed herself for Jessica's death. He could only imagine the torture she'd put herself through over the past few months.

"It didn't last, though," she went on, her voice still lacking luster. "A month later I had a nervous breakdown and spent two weeks in a mental hospital." One shoulder lifted in a seemingly nonchalant gesture. "I just never could go back after that."

The pain in her voice cut at Hal's soul like a sharpened razor. He found himself wishing he'd known her then, so he could have been there for her.

Finally, she looked back at him. "I'm sorry I didn't tell you about this before I examined Krista. You had a right to know, but there wasn't enough time. And I didn't want to put more stress on you than you were already dealing with."

"It's okay, Amy. You have nothing to apologize for."

One cynical brow inched up her forehead. "Oh? Are you saying if you had known about Jessica's death before I examined Krista, you wouldn't have hesitated before handing your daughter over to me?"

He thought for a moment. "I don't know."

"Well, at least you're honest," she said dryly.

Hal slid forward another inch or two. "Amy, I can't tell you what I would have done that night. I didn't even know you were a doctor before then. But now I do, and these past three days with you have shown me not only what a good physician you are, but what kind of person you are,"—he touched his fingertips to his chest—"right here." He shook his head. "I know you'd never do anything to hurt a child."

"But I did—"

"No, Amy, you didn't," he countered, his voice rising with conviction. "You were given the wrong file."

Her green eyes sparked with anger. "I was the doctor in charge that night, Hal. Jessica was my responsibility."

Hal noticed the firm set of her jaw and the stubborn glint in her eyes, and his respect for her doubled. Most people in her situation would have pointed the finger of blame elsewhere and gone along on their merry way, leaving the accused party, guilty or not, to suffer the consequences. But not Amy. She was determined to bear the responsibility for Jessica's death—alone.

Hal released a slow, labored sigh. He felt helpless. He wanted to do something to wipe the sadness from her face, erase the guilt and shame from her tortured conscience. But he didn't know how.

Help me, Lord. Show me what to do to make her see that only You hold the keys to life.

TELL HER I'M IN CONTROL, came the still, small Voice that so often directed Hal in times of confusion.

He rose, taking her cup from her and setting it on the coffee table. Then he kneeled in front of her and gathered her hands in his. "Amy, I don't know why Jessica died that night. But I do know you're not responsible."

She shook her head, rejecting his attempt to comfort her, and looked away.

Reaching up, Hal curled a finger beneath her chin and urged her to face him. "Listen to me, Amy. Suppose everything went exactly as it should have that night. Suppose the nurse had brought you the right file, and after talking to the little girl's mother you told her to bring Jessica in, and you did everything that doctors do for children having an asthma attack. How do you know Jessica would not have died anyway?"

"How do you know she would have?"

"Because God was in control of Jessica's destiny that night, Amy. Not you."

Amy flinched as though the finger still curled beneath her chin had shocked her.

Hal dropped his hand to the chair arm. "You do believe in God, don't you?"

She opened her mouth to respond, but no immediate words came.

Sensing a denial on the tip of her tongue, Hal held his breath in dreaded anticipation.

But the denial never came. Instead, an expression of anguish, followed by dazed bewilderment, crossed her delicate features and her gaze darted to the coffee table.

Hal knew she was looking at her Bible. Remembering what, he did not know. He wished he could read her mind, know the thoughts she was thinking, the memories she was recalling.

But he couldn't. All he could do was wait and pray that when her answer came, it would be what he wanted, what he needed to hear.

Finally, she shifted her eyes back to his. "Yes, Hal," she softly said, "I do believe in God."

Her humble confession sent Hal's heart soaring. He released a relieved breath.

"But—"

That one tiny word clipped a wing. "But?" he repeated, urging her on.

"I have to be honest with you, I'm having a difficult time with my faith right now."

"I understand," Hal told her honestly. He remembered a time in his life when he'd lost faith in both himself and God.

Tears pooled in her eyes. "I prayed that night, Hal," she said, her voice sounding as lost and forlorn as an orphaned child. "I asked God to let me reach Jessica on time, but He didn't. I got there just as the heart monitor went flat, and I couldn't revive her."

A visible tremor skipped across her body. She pursed her lips, obviously battling for self-control. "I'll never forget the look on that mother's face, her screams, the way she begged for God to have mercy."

Amy squeezed her eyes shut. Twin tears trailed down her cheeks. "Why, Hal? If God was in control that night, why wasn't He there for me? For Jessica? Why did an innocent child have to die because of my carelessness?"

Her tears ripped away the last of Hal's resistance. He slid his arms around her trembling body. She slipped her arms around his shoulders, grasping the back of his shirt in her fists. Then, burying her face in the crook of his shoulder, she released a heartrending sob.

Hal slid one hand up her spine and cupped the back of her head with his palm. Gently, he rocked her back and forth. Closing his eyes, he silently prayed.

Help her, Lord. Please take her pain away.

Little by little, her trembling ceased and her crying subsided. Hal gradually stopped rocking, and a calming stillness settled around them. After a while, she inhaled deeply then exhaled, releasing a shuddery sigh. Her feathery breath whispered against Hal's neck, cooling the moisture put there by her tears. Gooseflesh pricked the back of his neck and his arms tightened around her.

Conflicting emotions rose to do battle within him. His common sensibilities told him he should let her go, but his heart and soul told him he wanted to stay there and hold her this way forever.

Too soon, it seemed, she released the back of his shirt and withdrew from his embrace. Reluctantly, he let his hands fall heavily to the chair arms.

She wiped her face with the backs of her hands, then gingerly reached over and straightened his collar. With a small, chagrined smile, she said, "Sorry I got your shirt wet."

"That's okay." He reached up and brushed a wispy strand of hair away from her flushed cheek. "You can borrow my shoulder anytime you need to."

Her hand stilled, and so did his. Their gazes fused and, like a thrown power switch, a jolt of electricity surged between them. A breathless moment passed, then her gaze dropped to his mouth. She raised her hand from his collar and brushed feather-soft fingertips across his lips.

Desire, fierce and strong, shot through Hal. He wanted to pull her back into his arms again, breathe in her sweet scent, kiss her long, slender neck, feel her pulse beating beneath his lips. . . But a thin thread of rationality that had somehow remained intact warned him if he did, he'd cross a line neither of them was ready to cross.

Her raw vulnerability gave him the strength to stand and step back, putting much needed space between them.

Her eyes, wide and luminous, followed him as he rose, tugging at his emotions like a lighthouse beckoning a ship on a dark, stormy night. To be on the safe side, he stuffed his hands into his pockets.

He knew he should leave, but he couldn't with their conversation unfinished. There was more he needed to say to her about God's enduring love and mercy. But with her sitting there looking up at him that way, he didn't trust his own will power. He needed more air and space than the small living room provided.

"Would you walk with me outside?" he asked, not at all surprised by the huskiness in his own voice.

She nodded.

Hal waited while she slipped on her sandals, then followed her to the front door wiping tiny beads of perspiration from his brow. He hadn't felt this much like a flesh and blood man in a long time. A very long time.

When he stepped outside, he pulled the door closed behind them, firmly. The coolness hovering beneath the shade of the front porch brought blessed relief to his heated face. He drew in a deep, calming breath of the crisp air.

With her back to him, Amy stared thoughtfully at the mountains banking the meadow beyond her yard, then, crossing her arms, turned to him. "Hal, about my taking over as Krista's doctor—"

He pressed a finger to her lips. "Don't answer right now. Wait until you've had time to think about it."

She blinked in surprise. "You mean you still want me to be your daughter's doctor?"

He nodded. "Yeah. Whenever you're ready."

He found the feel of her soft pliant lips beneath his fingertip a bit too distracting and dropped his hand. Hooking his thumbs into his back pockets, he took a few seconds to weigh out his next words. He'd never considered himself much of a verbal witness for Christ before. Eloquent speeches and well-honed grammar skills were not among his strong suits. But, for some reason, this door had been opened to him, and he felt it was God's will he finish walking through it.

"Amy," Hal said at last, "you asked a while ago why God left you the night Jessica died."

Amy's gaze dropped to his chest, and Hal's confidence slipped a bit. The last thing he wanted to do was offend her, make her feel he was trying to preach a sermon.

TRUST ME, HAL, the still, small Voice reminded.

"I don't know why things happened like they did that night," Hal plunged forward. "But I do know that God didn't leave you. . .or Jessica."

She didn't speak, didn't raise her eyes.

"Think about it," Hal continued on. "Do you honestly think God would allow an innocent child to die because of someone else's mistake?"

Her gaze darted back to his. Something he said had apparently captured her attention.

"Of course, He wouldn't," Hal said in answer to his own question. "He's not that kind of God." In a softer, gentler voice, he added, "He loves you, Amy. He only wants what's best for you."

She tucked her right lower lip between her teeth, and shifted her weight from one leg to the other. "I hear what you're saying, Hal. It's just that. . ." She glanced away, her ponderous thoughts hanging heavy between them.

Hal searched his mind for something else to say, something that would erase the doubt and confusion etched on her lovely face. But no more words of Divine wisdom came. So he just waited.

Finally, she looked back. Uncrossing her arms, she inched forward and laid a palm against his chest. Of its own volition, his hand rose to cover hers.

"Thank you, Hal," she said, "for listening, and for your words of encouragement. You've given me a lot to think about." She searched his face for a fleeting few seconds, then added, "I mean that."

And somehow, Hal knew she did. Smiling, he squeezed her hand and was rewarded with a soft smile in return.

It was now time to go. He had said all God wanted him to say. He had no other excuse to prolong his stay. Stepping back, he broke the contact between them. "I guess I'd better run."

"Yes," she said, recrossing her arms. "You'll want to be there when Krista wakes up."

Hal paused, taking in Amy's lovely features. She was like a beaming light at the end of a long dark tunnel. The closer he got to her, the brighter she shined.

"Amy," he felt compelled to add, "anytime you need to talk, just let me know. I may not have many of the answers you're looking for, but I can always listen."

"I'll keep that in mind."

With a "See you later," he turned and headed for his SUV. Before sliding beneath the steering wheel, he looked back toward the front porch, intending to send Amy one final wave good-bye. But to his disappointment, she'd already slipped inside and closed the door.

ten

As soon as Hal turned and walked away, Amy slipped inside and closed the door, berating herself for falling apart in front of him. She hated losing self-control. It was an arduous reminder of how volatile and unpredictable her emotions had become, how far removed she was from the confident, self-assured doctor she'd been just a few short months ago.

Odd, she thought as she wandered back to the living room. She'd known when she'd chosen a career in pediatrics it would be a long, slow climb to the top. But she'd never once stopped to consider what a fast, hard fall it could be to the bottom. Or how difficult it would be to get up when she got there.

She slumped down on the sofa, mentally and physically drained. Not surprising, considering extreme exhaustion always followed an emotional visit to her not so distant past.

How did people like Hal do it? Maintain their unwavering faith in God even in the face of a crisis, like the one he'd recently experienced with Krista.

Amy propped her elbows on her knees and her chin on her fists, thinking back on the last three days she'd spent with Hal. Every evening, without fail, he'd read from the Gideon Bible placed in Krista's hospital room. More than once he'd visited the hospital chapel to pray. He'd even told another couple, practical strangers, that he'd pray for their daughter's speedy recovery from pneumonia.

Yet not once had she heard him say anything or react in any way to indicate he blamed God for his daughter's rare blood disorder—a malady she may have to deal with for a long time.

Obviously, he was a man of devout faith, a man who depended on Divine Authority rather than his own, a man at peace with himself. . .and with God.

A thread of envy wove through her. "How do you do it, Hal?" she muttered. "What's your secret?"

When he'd asked her if she believed in God, she'd almost said "Not anymore." But then she'd stopped and thought about the acrimony and bitterness she'd lived with for the past three and a half months and decided yes, she did still believe in God. How could she not believe in Someone she was so angry with?

But Hal's relationship with God, she suspected, went beyond belief.

She ran her fingertips across her forehead, trying to dissuade the dull throb building there. A mental picture of Hal sitting in the corner of Krista's hospital room, reading the Gideon Bible floated through her mind. Her eyes shifted to her own Bible lying on the coffee table. Robert had given her the testament on her sixteenth birthday, shortly after she'd made a commitment to follow Christ. She'd felt so close to God then, so cherished and loved. But somewhere between then and now, all that had changed, and, in all honesty, it had started long before Jessica's death.

Leaning forward, she picked up the white, leather-bound book. How long had it been since she'd used God's Word for something other than a table decoration? Weeks? Months? Guilt pierced her conscience. No, it hadn't been weeks or even months since her daily devotions ended. But years. She truthfully didn't know how long. She'd lost track. Her life had become so busy. . .

The shock of realization hit her full force and shame washed over her. Yes, her life had been busy. Too busy to include God.

Tears blurred her vision as the reason for all her pain, confusion, and loneliness became startlingly clear. God had not left her; she had left Him.

She hugged the Bible to her chest, and a life-changing warmth spread through her, like the Book sprouted wings and hugged her back. She may not know what she was going to do with her life and where she was headed, but she did know, wherever that was, she didn't want to go there without God.

Closing her eyes, she bowed her head and, for the first time since Jessica's death, and only the second time since she could remember, Amy prayed.

❧

The ax fell full force against the wood, splitting the fire log into two even halves and launching them in opposite directions. Hal bent, picking up the piece of timber that had landed nearest him, then stood it upright on the large round stump he used for a chopping block.

The damp night air and the sweat seeping from his pores merged on the surface of his skin, wrapping his bare upper body in cool, dank clamminess.

Glowing from the back corners of his house, flood lamps cast long, eerie shadows across the yard. And beyond the beaming lights, in the stillness of the forest, crickets sang a rhythmic, peaceful song.

Peace, Hal thought with another deliberate swing of the ax. That's what he'd come out here seeking. But with each smack of the blade, and each ear-shattering separation of wood, he only became more confused.

Seemed like Fate was determined to make Dr. Amelia Nicole Jordan an imminent part of his life. And feelings beyond his control had already granted her a continuous place in his thoughts, a constant presence in his dreams.

He liked her. Not just how she looked, but how she walked, how she talked, how she laughed. How she touched a place inside him no one had ever touched before—not even Adrienne.

And that realization, staring him square in the face, scared him to death.

Falling in love may feel great. But falling out could cut a man's soul so deep that only the healing power of God could close the wounds. And nothing could take away the scars, those ugly, deeply embedded reminders of what can happen when you give too much of yourself to someone.

"Hal Cooper, put your shirt back on before you catch your

death of cold."

Glancing over his shoulder, he found his mother, wrapped in a terry robe, her feet tucked into untied hiking boots, standing several yards behind him. In each hand she balanced a heavy ceramic mug.

"Hi, Mom." He leaned the ax against the chopping block and reached for the shirt he'd tossed over the back of a nearby lawn chair. Slipping first one arm and then the other through the sleeves, he grinned at her, silently telling her he didn't take her scolding seriously, but would do as she ordered simply to appease her, because he loved her.

She waited until he'd buttoned the last button, then passed a mug to him. The hearty scent of strong black coffee rose to tempt his senses.

Ellen studied the diminishing wood pile, then shifted her gaze to two waist-high rows of split fire logs Hal had neatly stacked on the opposite side of the chopping block. "Goodness," she said, "I don't think we've ever been so well prepared for winter."

Yes, Hal could argue, they had. Once. That week almost five years ago when he'd finally agreed to give Adrienne a divorce. The same week she'd died alongside her newest lover in a single-engine plane crash.

"Do you want to go inside?" he asked his mother. "It's kind of chilly out here."

She looked up, where a half moon and a brilliant canopy of stars illuminated the midnight blue sky. "No. It's such a beautiful night. Let's sit out here a few minutes."

She eased down into the lawn chair. Hal settled on the chopping block.

After taking one generous sip of coffee, he leaned forward, elbows on knees, cupping the warm mug in his hands. "I hope my wood chopping didn't wake you."

"You woke me, Hal, but it wasn't your wood chopping."

Hal quirked his brows in question.

"You're my son," she answered his silent query. "I always

know when something's troubling you."

Hal wasn't surprised. He and his mother were close. She knew him better than anyone else. And he knew there was no point in dancing around the issue. She'd probably already figured out what was bothering him.

He focused on the steam rising from his mug. "It's Amy."

"Oh?"

"I like her."

"What's not to like. She's beautiful, generous, intelligent. . ."

He met her gaze. "I like her. . .a lot."

His mother's eyes filled with understanding. "I see." Several pensive seconds ticked by. "Any idea how she feels about you?"

Hal nodded. "I think there's something there."

"But you're afraid."

Again, he nodded.

Ellen leaned forward, elbows on knees. "Hal, Amy is very different from Adrienne."

"I know, Mom." *Now,* he added to himself. "Even so, I've got a lot to consider before entering into a relationship. . .with anybody."

"Such as."

"Well, Krista for one." He shook his head. "I don't want her to get hurt. And that's exactly what will happen if Amy steps into our lives and then, for some reason, walks out."

"Like Adrienne did."

A distant but all-too-clear memory rose up to taunt Hal. Krista had been six months old the last time Adrienne had walked out. Too young to understand that her mother didn't want her. But Krista was older now. What would it do to her should she fall in love with Amy then lose her?

"Hal," his mother said, "I don't want Krista to get hurt either. And if I felt that were going to happen, I'd be the first to state my opinion."

Hal stared into the darkness beyond the yard, where crickets continued to chirp and an owl released a lonely sounding *hoot-hoot.* For a heartbeat, he wished he could erase twenty or so years. Go back to a time when his life was much simpler, when deciding what was best for him was someone else's responsibility. Finally, he said, "How can I know for sure, Mom?"

"You can't. Life holds no guarantees."

"It's not worth the risks, then."

"Are you sure about that?"

Yes, he was sure. . .he thought. But, for some reason, he couldn't voice that conviction to his mother. He felt her touch his knee and looked back at her.

"Sometimes, Son, when you feel God leading you in a new direction, you have to step out on faith and trust Him to take care of your loved ones."

A silent understanding passed between them. How many times had she, during his tumultuous marriage, stepped out on faith, trusting God to take care of Hal and his family? Only she and God knew.

Patting his knee, Ellen stood and drew back her shoulders as though shaking off the dismal mood. "I'm going back to bed, and I suggest you do the same. It's just a few hours until sunrise." With that, she turned and headed back to the house, leaving Hal with his thoughts.

The wind whispered by, slipped inside the porous material of his shirt, and fingered a chill across his skin. Trust God, his mother had said. Hal thought he could do that. But what about Amy? Could she learn to trust God again?

Hal would not consider a future with anyone who didn't share his faith. He'd made that mistake once, and it'd cost him—dearly. So for now, it seemed, all he could be to Amy was a friend.

Standing, he dumped his cold coffee on the ground and set the mug next to the chair. Reaching in the woodpile, he grabbed a log and stood it upright on the chopping block. Then, wrapping first one hand and then the other around the ax handle, he continued splitting wood.

eleven

Later that morning, Hal slid into a booth at Grace's Café across from Amy. She'd phoned him as he was headed out the door for work and asked him if he could meet her for breakfast. Said she had something she wanted to tell him.

Hal suspected her invitation had something to do with their conversation the night before. He'd told her to call anytime she needed someone to talk to, and he'd meant it. Still, hearing her voice when he'd picked up the receiver that morning surprised him. He hadn't expected to hear from her so soon.

"Thanks for coming, Hal," she said, folding the newspaper she'd been reading and laying it on the seat beside her.

"No problem."

She asked about Krista and his mother, and he told her they were both doing fine, but Krista was a little disappointed she couldn't return to school this week. She loved kindergarten.

The waitress came and took their order, and as she walked away, Amy leaned forward on her forearms. "I asked you to come this morning, Hal, because I wanted to thank you."

He arched his brows. "Thank me?"

"Yes. . .for what you said last night. After you left, it didn't take long for me to realize that you were right. God hadn't left me. He'd been there all along, waiting for me to return to Him."

Hal leaned forward, matching Amy's position. Could this mean what he thought? "Go on," he urged.

"I'd let so many things come between me and God. School, my studies, my practice. . ."

The waitress brought their coffee, but Hal hardly noticed.

"When I first began praying last night," Amy continued. "I thought it'd take a while for me to get through to God. You

120

know, gain His forgiveness. But it didn't. I asked, and right there He was, waiting to answer." The corners of her mouth turned up softly, and Hal noticed for the first time since he'd met her, her smile reached her eyes. "God's given me a second chance to live my life for Him. I intend to do it right this time. Not fail Him like I did before."

She reached over and covered his hand with her own. "I just wanted to share that with you, Hal, and let you know what you said last night made a difference."

He turned over his hand and wove his fingers with hers. "I'm glad you did, Amy. You have no idea what that means to me." *No idea,* he added to himself.

They sat there holding hands, talking about her newfound faith, until their food arrived. While they ate, their conversation wandered to more general topics: the weather, their work, the upcoming Harvest Festival.

About halfway through the meal, which neither of them seemed particularly interested in, Amy glanced at her watch and gasped. "Oh dear! I'm going to be late for work."

She reached for the check, but Hal beat her to it, stuffing the slip of paper into his shirt pocket.

"I don't have time to argue with you, Hal Cooper," she scolded good-naturedly. "But the next one's on me."

Outside, he walked her to her car and opened the door for her. Before slipping beneath the steering wheel, she turned to him with another radiant smile. "Thanks again, Hal. You're a good friend."

Hal drove to work a little in awe of what Amy had told him. She'd made peace with God, which meant she was now equally yoked with Hal in faith.

The main obstacle standing between him and Amy had just fallen away.

Hal felt like he'd just been given the green light, a "go-ahead" signal from God to take his and Amy's relationship one step further. And that's exactly what he intended to do.

He rolled down his window and folded his arm over the

door. Talk about an answered prayer. God had been a few steps ahead of Hal on this one.

ટ

"Come in," Amy called in response to the knock on her office door Friday afternoon.

The door swung open and a curly-haired bundle of energy sprinted toward her.

"Miss Amy!"

"Krista!"

The sight of the child sent a bolt of joy through Amy. She rolled away from her desk and swiveled sideways just in time to scoop the resilient tyke up onto her lap. Inconspicuously, she examined the child's arms. The bruises had faded to a pale greenish purple, and she saw no new discoloration. A good sign.

Krista gave Amy an enthusiastic hug, which Amy returned. Then, in one quick motion, Krista planted her small hands on Amy's shoulders and pushed back, looking up at Amy with blue eyes stretched wide with excitement. "Me an' Daddy's got a surprise for you."

"For me?"

"Uh-huh." Krista's head bobbed up and down.

Amy looked toward the open doorway, where Hal leaned with one shoulder against the frame, his thumbs hooked in his back pockets, looking like a heavenly dream. He dazzled her with a broad smile that dimpled both cheeks. For about the space of four heartbeats, Amy forgot to breathe.

"Tell me, Doc," he said. "Why do women have such a hard time keeping secrets?" There was a teasing note in his voice, a lightheartedness she'd never noticed before.

She tried to think of a quick-witted comeback, but his presence had scattered her senses. "I don't know," she finally managed to mumble, then wanted to kick herself for sounding like a bumbling idiot.

"Show her the 'prise, Daddy," an impatient Krista urged.

He shoved away from the door frame and reached behind

the exterior wall, withdrawing a large, framed. . .something. Amy couldn't tell what, with him holding it down by his side.

Stepping forward, he lifted and turned the frame so that Amy could see and her mouth dropped open in surprise. Inside the smoothly finished oak casing was the completed picture Amy had asked Krista to draw for the office wall.

Amy reached out and ran her fingertips across the polished wood, then over the non-glare glass protecting the picture. "It's beautiful."

"I helped Daddy make it for you," Krista said.

Amy lifted her gaze to Hal's. "You guys made this?"

He gave a modest shrug.

A warm glow coiled in Amy's chest and unbidden tears stung her eyes. She'd received her share of gifts in the past. Expensive trinkets and frivolous commodities bought without thought or sentiment. But no one had ever taken the time or gone to the trouble to make something for her with their own hands.

"Do you like it, Miss Amy?" Krista wanted to know.

Amy blinked the moisture away. "I love it. It's the best present I've ever received," she said, and meant it.

Krista beamed, and Amy felt a maternal tug on her heartstrings. Why did this pair have such an enchanting affect on her?

"Can we hang it up now?" Krista asked.

"Sure," Amy said. "Let me go see if I can find a hammer and some nails in the supply closet."

"I've already got it covered." From his back pocket, Hal withdrew a child-sized hammer and a small plastic bag of picture hangers.

"Well, aren't you Mr. Resourceful," Amy said without thought.

He wiggled his brows. "I try to be."

Amy blinked in surprise. Was he flirting with her? Or had she imagined it? She swallowed nervously and wet her lips. "Okay. Let's get started." Setting Krista on her feet, Amy stood on legs that felt a bit like jelly.

Ten minutes later, they all stood back and admired the new addition to Amy's office. In the picture, three stick people and a stick creature of some sort stood side by side between a house with a chimney and a tree.

Amy lifted Krista to her hip. "Tell me about the people in the picture."

Pointing, Krista said, "That's Daddy, and that's me, and that's you."

"Me?"

"Uh-huh."

But, Amy thought it was. . ."Where's your grandmother?"

"She's in the house, cookin' chicken for the picnic."

"Oh," Amy replied, not allowing herself to contemplate why she herself was included in the picture. She pointed to the stick creature. "Who's this?"

"That's Rufkin."

Of course, Amy should have remembered the dog.

The door cracked open and Linda poked her head inside. "Want to get a treat from the Treasure Chest, Krista?" Every child who visited the clinic was rewarded with a trip to Dr. Robert's treasure chest of toys and treats.

"Yes!" Krista said, squirming for release.

Amy set Krista on her feet and, in a split instant, the child was gone.

After the door closed behind Krista and Linda, Amy turned to Hal. "How did the checkup go?"

"Great. Krista's platelet count is up to one hundred fifty-three thousand."

"That's the best news I've heard all day."

"Me, too." Hal leaned back against the wall, apparently in no hurry to leave. "I asked Robert if I could take her on a picnic tomorrow."

"What did he say?"

"To ask you."

Mentally, Amy planned a slow session of torture for Robert.

He knew very well that Krista could return to normal activity with a platelet count of one hundred fifty-three thousand. He'd asked Amy's advice on the child's limitations that very morning.

Amy didn't mind sharing her knowledge of ITP with Robert, but she had asked him to keep her involvement in Krista's case behind the scenes. Lot of good that request had done.

Feeling she'd been given little choice but to answer Hal's question, Amy leaned back against the desk. "A picnic sounds fine, Hal. As you know, Krista's platelet count has returned to normal. However, you do need to keep her out of trees and off bicycles for a while, away from anything where there's a risk of head injury. At least until you're sure the ITP isn't going to reoccur."

Hal looked perplexed. "That's not going to be easy."

Amy's lips tipped. "I know." Krista's liveliness could drain the stamina of a world-class athlete.

"What about you, Doc?" Hal asked. "Want to come along?"

The invitation caught Amy off guard. "You want me to come?"

"Sure," he responded, as though asking her to a picnic was an everyday occurrence. "That is, if you'd like to."

If she'd like to. Of course, she would. But, *should* she? Every minute she spent with Hal she lost another little piece of her heart.

She glanced at a generous but neatly stacked pile of paperwork on her desk. "I really should work tomorrow." Inwardly she cringed at how lame her excuse sounded, like she'd intentionally left the door wide open in hopes that he'd ask again. Why hadn't she simply told him she *was* going to work tomorrow, as she'd intended to do before she opened her mouth?

"Aw, come on, Doc," Hal said. "Surely after spending three days cooped up with us in the hospital this week, you could use a break, too."

The guileless plea in his voice and the boyishly charming expression on his face beat down Amy's feeble resistance and steered her thoughts in another direction. What could one little picnic hurt? A friendly family outing to celebrate Krista's quick recovery.

"Well, what do you say?" Hal cajoled. "Is it a date?"

Her heart took off in a giddy sprint across her breastbone. "Sure. What time should I be ready?"

His grin broadened, and Amy allowed herself to believe he was thoroughly pleased she'd accepted his invitation.

"How does ten sound? That way, we can get in a little fishing before we eat."

"Sounds great," Amy said, even though she had never been fishing in her life. He'd probably have to show her which end of the pole to hold.

He pushed away from the wall and tucked his fingers into his jeans' pockets. "Well, I guess I'd better go find Krista. Linda probably needs rescuing by now."

"Okay."

"Well, I'll see you tomorrow, Doc." He headed for the door.

"Hal," she said as he reached for the doorknob.

He looked back at her.

"I wish you wouldn't call me 'Doc.'"

He winked at her. "Anything you say, Doc." With that, he opened the door and slipped through it.

Amy looked heavenward and shook her head.

Then she stood staring at the space he'd just vacated. Something had definitely changed in him. Before, he'd always been intensely serious, cautiously guarded where she was concerned with what Amy thought of as a *you-can-get-close-but-not-too-close* mentality. But today, that shield had dropped, and she couldn't help wondering why.

Shaking her head, she circled her desk and sat down. He was obviously thrilled Krista had gotten such a good report. That was all. What caring father wouldn't be elated to hear his daughter could return to normal activities when she'd been in the hospital a few short days ago?

Amy pulled up patient accounts on her computer, then glared absently at the screen, unable to dispel the sanguine thoughts swirling through her mind. Hal had teased and joked with her. *Flirted* with her. She was sure of it. And Hal Cooper was not a man who made amorous advances lightly. Amy knew, because he'd had at least a dozen opportunities to do so while Krista was in the hospital. Practically every pediatric nurse that had visited the child's room, both young and aged, had taken their turn at trying to impress him with coquettish looks, impudent giggles, and seductively swaying hips.

But, like a granite statue, Hal had remained unimpressed. Either that or he'd done a very good job at covering up his interests.

Now, here he was cracking carefree jokes and winking at her—harmless gestures had they come from someone other than the usually serious and brooding lumberjack. Plus, he'd asked her to go with him on a picnic, then referred to the outing as a date. Amy worried her right lower lip with her teeth. Good report on Krista aside, something had changed.

The screen saver popped on, throwing a multitude of shooting stars in Amy's direction. She swiveled away from the computer and propped her elbows on her desk, plopping her chin in one hand. A despondent sigh slipped past her lips. "What's going on here, Lord?"

She didn't receive an answer, but she really wasn't listening for one. She had her own ideas about what was happening between her and Hal. Something wonderful and exciting. . .

And. . .

Possibly impossible, she reminded herself, jerking her thoughts out of the castle in the air they'd drifted into. A disgruntled frown creased her forehead. She had no business engaging in romantic fantasies about Hal until she figured out what she was going to do with the rest of her life.

She turned back to the computer, striking a key that banished the shooting stars from the screen. In all fairness, she should tell Hal just how uncertain her future was before their ill-timed attraction for each other evolved into something more.

She glanced at the door. He was probably still at the clinic. She could go find him and tell him she'd changed her mind about the picnic, decided not to go, nip a possible romance in the bud before it got off the ground floor.

Or, she could wait and see how the outing went, just in case she was reading more into his sudden effervescence than what was really there.

Amy drummed her fingers on her desk. Keep the date or cancel. What should she do? She weighed the decision in the balances a few more deliberating seconds, then turned to her computer and went back to work.

twelve

"Whoa, Doc!"

Hal captured Amy's wrist, thwarting her attempt to throw her line back out into the gently flowing waters of Cedar Creek, the watercourse for which the town Cedar Creek was named.

Amy looked behind her to see if her line was tangled in the drooping branches. When she saw her hook dangling idly at the end of her rod, she looked at Hal and frowned. "What's wrong?"

"I'm hungry," he said, "and before I untangle one more hook from one more tree, I need to eat."

Her frown turned into a scowl. "If I remember correctly, this was your idea."

"I know. But now I have a better idea." He started peeling her fingers from around the rod. "It's called 'lunch.' "

Reluctantly and with a small degree of disappointment, she released the pole. She never realized fishing could be such fun.

Of course, it probably hadn't been much of a treat for Hal. He'd moved her to three different locations along the creek bank. Still, about every other cast, she somehow managed to get her line tangled in some obtrusive form of plant life. So he'd spent the better part of the morning untangling rather than fishing.

Poor man. No wonder he looked so frazzled.

He laid aside Amy's rod and turned to Krista, who stood a couple of yards away, ankle-deep in water, her own child-sized pole clutched in her hands. Intently, she watched her line, waiting for the slightest nip or tug that would indicate she'd snagged a fish.

It dawned on Amy that Krista hadn't once needed her father's assistance. "Do you suppose I'll ever get the hang of it?"

She hadn't realized she'd voiced her thoughts until Hal glanced back at her. "Sure, you will. It just takes a little time and practice." His response was polite enough, but, considering his finger-combed hair and haggard expression, he was probably thinking, *Lots of time. Lots of practice.*

He turned his attention back to his daughter. "Time for lunch, Buttercup."

Krista, her face framed with corkscrew curls that had escaped her pigtails, looked up at her father with moping eyes. "But, I want to fish some more."

"I know, and you can. After we eat." Hal's words, while gentle, brooked no argument.

Lower lip protruding in an artful pout, Krista reeled in her line.

The day had turned out to be the perfect one for a picnic. The wind was calm and the air full of sights and sounds of nature: whistling songbirds, barking squirrels, the swish-gurgle of the crystalline stream.

Amy spread a wedding-ring quilt in the shade of an ancient oak while Hal hauled the picnic basket from the car. "Can I help?" she asked, reaching for the lid when Hal set the basket down.

He brushed away her hand. "Nope. You're our guest. That means we serve you."

Feeling a bit useless, she sat back while Hal and Krista started pulling out food and arranging it on the quilt. The father-daughter pair uncovered fried chicken, potato salad, green beans, corn-on-the-cob, and rolls. And if that wasn't enough, an apple pie—fresh baked from the looks and smell of it—and a frosty pitcher of tea.

"Wow!" Amy said, her mouth watering. "Did you cook all this?"

"I wish I could take the credit," Hal said. "But I had Sal down at Grace's Café whip up the potato salad and apple pie."

Amy narrowed her eyes suspiciously. "Your mom didn't have a hand in this? Not even the chicken?"

"Unfortunately, no. She's tied up at a church yard sale today. So, I'm afraid you're stuck with my cooking."

"Well, you shouldn't have gone to so much trouble."

He stopped short of handing a stack of napkins to Krista and captured Amy's gaze with his own. "I wanted to," he said softly.

Amy's breath caught in her throat. She tried to glance down or look away, but she couldn't escape the hypnotic pull of his intense chestnut eyes. The birds still sang, the squirrels still barked, and the brook still gurgled. But, for one breathless moment, it seemed, time stood still.

"Dad-*dy*, hand me the napkins."

Krista's impetuous voice broke the enchanting spell. Amy finally managed to drop her gaze and Hal went back to arranging food fit for a southern governor's dining table.

Hardly ten minutes into the meal, Krista set her plate aside and wiped her mouth with a napkin. "Can I go fish some more, Daddy?"

"You've hardly touched your food," he pointed out.

Krista folded her arms over her stomach and filtered a laborious sigh, like she'd just finished her third helping of a Thanksgiving feast. "But, I'm full."

"Okay," Hal relented. "You can go on and fish some more, but stay on the shore until Amy and I get back down there."

Wise move on Hal's part, Amy thought. It caused more grief than glory to force a child to eat when he or she wasn't hungry or interested.

The child's doleful expression blossomed into a brilliant smile. With the buoyancy of a prima ballerina, she jumped up and skipped down to the stream, her curly pigtails bouncing along behind her.

Concern creased Hal's brow as he watched his daughter flutter away. "You know, I worry sometimes about her not eating enough."

Hal's anxiety spawned a sense of servitude in Amy, nudged her to do what she was trained to do, what once came so naturally for her. She reached over and laid a hand on his knee.

His skin, exposed by the denim shorts he wore, felt warm beneath her palm.

When he looked at her, she gave him a reassuring smile. "Krista's fine, Hal. She'll eat when she's hungry."

Hal shook his head. "You sound like Robert."

"Well, Robert's right. She's healthy and happy. As long as she doesn't lose weight, she'll be fine. She is a little petite, but I suspect that's hereditary."

"Yes. Her mother was small. Five-two."

"There you go, then. I hate to have to break this to you, but you've got one perfectly normal child."

He grinned sheepishly. "I still worry about her, though." He hunched one shoulder. "I can't help it."

She patted his knee. "Spoken like a true father."

Turning her attention back to the food, she dug into a bowl for a piece of chicken, settling for a leg. She was about to sink her teeth into the first bite when she felt him watching her. Slanting him a glance, she found him grinning, his brown eyes dancing with laughter.

She closed her mouth and waved the drumstick at him in a mock threat. "Don't you dare say one word about my appetite, Hal Cooper. I've never tried it, but I think I could pack a pretty powerful wallop with this chicken leg if provoked."

Hal held up a hand in surrender. "Hey, you'll not hear me mention that that's your second piece of chicken, or that you've already finished off two helpings of potato salad."

She narrowed her eyes. "Bet I can still beat you down to the river."

One dark brow rose in amusement. "You think so?"

"I *know* so."

"Okay. On three."

Amy set her plate down. So did Hal. While they scrambled up off the ground, their gazes remained locked, each gauging the other's movements.

"One," Amy said slowly, taking the initiative in starting the count. Then, without warning, she took off running, tossing a quick "two-three" back over her shoulder.

"Hey!" Hal called after her. "That's cheating!"

Halfway to the river, she glanced back and found him close on her heels. She squealed and picked up speed. But just as she reached the water, his arm snaked around her waist. In one fluid motion, he bent and came up with her cradled in his arms. She hooked her arms around his neck.

"You cheated," Hal repeated. "And for that, you're gonna pay."

Krista, who'd abandoned her fishing pole, danced around them, clapping her hands. "Do it, Daddy! Do it!"

Amy looked from the rakish lumberjack, to the child, then back to the lumberjack, who suddenly reminded her of a wolf, a magnificent creature of the wild that had just captured some unsuspecting prey.

"Do what?" she asked, her voice small and totally void of the brazen confidence she'd possessed less than two minutes ago when she'd first issued the challenge.

"When you don't play fair, you get dunked."

Her confidence returned. "Oh, yeah, right." She was fully clothed in shorts, shirt, and shoes. So was he. He wasn't going to dunk her.

He stepped into the water.

Then, again, he might.

Her momentary cocky self-assuredness fled like a scared rabbit. Unlooping her arms from his neck, she braced her palms on his shoulders. "Come on, Hal. You don't want to get wet."

He merely curled his arms tighter around her. "Says who?"

"Does my opinion count?"

"Huh-uh." He stepped farther out into the water.

Amy continued to struggle, but pushing against Hal's chest was like trying to move Stone Mountain. "Come on, Hal. I have on new shoes."

"I'll buy you another pair."

"Can't. They're one-of-a-kind. Tailor-made."

His cocky grin tipped sideways. "Yeah, right. They're canvas. Very rare."

Amy looked down. Hal was thigh-deep and sinking with each step. He was going to do it. He was really going to dunk her. And that water was ice-bucket cold. In an act of desperation, she flung her arms around his neck and buried her face against him. "Okay, lumberjack. I go down. You go down."

"Have it your way, Doc." With that, he plunged beneath the frigid water.

The chill shocked her. Struggling not to gasp—which could result in her swallowing one of the scaly creatures swimming below the creek's surface—she tightened her hold on Hal.

He released her legs and slipped his arms around her waist. Then, with her body clasped tightly against his, he brought her back up.

They stood a moment holding onto each other, trying to catch their breath. Then, drawing back, Amy raked the hair away from her face and scowled at Hal, who looked tremendously pleased with himself.

"Are you happy now?" she asked, trying to sound disgruntled. Not an easy thing to do with laughter bubbling up from her chest, threatening escape.

The merriment in his eyes faded. His gaze dropped to her lips, then rose again to her eyes. "Yeah, Doc," he answered, his voice husky. "I'd say I'm pretty happy right now."

Amy's frozen body thawed in a heartbeat. She became acutely aware of his warm breath caressing her face, the rise and fall of his chest with every breath he took, his hand pressing against the small of her back.

Kiss me, she thought. *Kiss me and watch me disintegrate into a million brilliant pieces.*

"Dunk me, now, Daddy. It's my turn."

Krista's voice, although coming from the nearby shore, sounded faint and far away.

"We need to talk," Hal said.

"I know," Amy whispered.

"Tonight?" His brows rose question. "I'll ask Mom to watch Krista."

Amy nodded.

Hal released her and turned his attention toward his daughter. "Okay, Buttercup, you ready to get wet?"

Krista jumped up and down, squealing with delight.

"Wait," Amy said before Hal took his second step toward the creek bank. "You forgot something."

Hal glanced over at Amy as she stepped up beside him. "What?"

"Just this." She looped an arm across his chest, kicked his feet out from under him, and pushed him under. She was halfway to the cove when he popped up, giving her a wicked "I'll get you back" look.

She shot him an impish grin and headed for the quilt. She couldn't wait to see how he intended to "get her back."

After packing the food away and setting aside the picnic basket, she pulled the quilt around her shoulders then sat, watching father and daughter. Amid the child's squeals of laughter and shrieks of delight, Hal would dip under water with her, then he'd allow her to dunk him.

What a relationship, Amy thought. Would Krista, as she grew, come to realize how blessed she was to have a father like Hal? Not an action, thought, or decision was made without consideration of his daughter.

The scene opened up a bittersweet trail leading back to her own childhood. She remembered being Krista's age, the nights she fell asleep holding the book her father never got home in time to read, the dance recitals he missed, the birthday parties he never made on time. . .or forgot altogether.

Amy shook her head, forcing her thoughts back to the present, chiding herself for venturing down memory lane. When she'd rededicated her life to Christ, she'd promised herself to let go of the past and stay focused on the future—whatever that future may be.

Something pricked Amy's awareness. A sound, faint yet

urgent, muffled by the gurgle of the stream and Hal and Krista's laughter. Frowning, Amy tipped her head, straining to hear.

"Help! Somebody! Please, help! Anybody! Please!"

Gooseflesh raced down Amy's arms. Someone was in trouble, and, if she wasn't mistaken, the voice belonged to a child. Adrenaline kicking in, she threw off the blanket and jumped up. "Hal!"

The frolicking stopped as both father and daughter looked at Amy.

"Someone's in trouble downstream. I'm going to see what's going on."

"Wait," Hal said. "I'll go with you."

But Amy was already sprinting toward the desperate young voice. She knew when help was needed, milliseconds mattered—could even make the difference between life and death.

She tackled a dense area of growth, slapping branches out of her way, plowing through the low-growing foliage clawing at her ankles. "Hang on! I'm coming. Hang on!"

When she finally broke through to a small clearing, the sight before her threatened to stop her in her tracks, but pure gut instinct and inborn ineptness propelled her forward.

A boy around the age of ten kneeled on the creek bank. In front of him, on the rocky ground, lay another boy, perhaps a couple of years younger. He was pale and lifeless, with a pool of blood forming at the top of his head.

Amy fell to her knees on the opposite side of the injured child. "What happened?" she asked the older boy while she took a quick glance at the scarlet soil above the younger child's blond hair to gain a vague idea of how much blood had been lost.

"He–he's my br–brother," the older child managed to croak past his sobs. "I think he's dead."

While the boy explained, Amy checked his brother's breathing and found none. She tilted back his head, covered his mouth with her own, and blew.

His chest rose and fell.

She checked for a pulse. Faint but steady. "What's your name?" she asked the older child while watching, praying the younger child's chest would rise and fall on its own. It didn't. She gave another breath.

"Joey," the boy answered.

When Amy raised up to gauge the rise and fall of the child's chest, Hal was there, kneeling beside her. "Heaven help, Joey," he said. "What happened to Timmy?"

Timmy, Amy repeated to herself. Good. She had his name.

She watched Timmy's thin chest, silently willing an unprovoked rise and fall of the child's rib cage.

"H–he dived off the rocks," Joey explained. "I dared him, but I didn't think he'd really do it." A heartrending sob tore from his throat. "I killed him, Hal. I think I killed my brother!"

"You didn't kill you brother, Joey," Amy heard Hal tell the child. "You probably saved his life by getting him out of the water."

Amy hoped, prayed Joey had gotten his brother out in time. She gave another breath. Timmy's chest rose and fell, then, again, nothing. *Help me, Lord. If it be Your will, help me save this child.* "Come on, Timmy," she muttered, willing the child to fight for his life. "Breathe for me, baby. Breathe." She bent to supply him with another breath, but stopped when he drew in a deep breath on his own.

"He's breathing," she said, more for the benefit of his brother than anyone else. Timmy's eyes fluttered open, and Amy felt the sharp sting of tears. She batted the moisture away. At the moment, she didn't have the time or luxury to cry.

"Hold his legs, Hal." She placed a firm hand on each of the child's shoulders. "We've got to keep him as still and calm as possible until I can check him out."

As anticipated, fear leapt into Timmy's blue eyes and he started to struggle against them.

"Listen to me, Sparky," she said in a firm but controlled voice. "You're hurt, but you're going to be fine." Still, the child struggled. "Your brother is here with you, and so are your friends Hal and Krista."

"That's right, Buddy," Hal said. "I'm right here. We're going to take care of you."

The struggle ebbed a bit.

Joey reached over and placed a hand on Timmy's shoulder. "Me, too, Timmy. I'm here."

At the sound of his brother's voice, the struggling ceased.

"An' me, too, Timmy," came another small voice. "I'm here, too."

Amy glanced sideways and, for the first time since running upon the injured child, noticed Krista. She kneeled at Timmy's feet, patting his ankle. Amy would smile about the precious scene later, when she knew Timmy was out of danger.

She turned her attention back to the patient.

A scowl creased his forehead. "Who are you?" he asked bluntly.

"My name is Amy. I'm a doctor." She watched his eyes, his breathing, and his head, which was still oozing blood. She held her hand out to Hal. "Give me your shirt."

He did as she requested, and she placed the shirt against the two-inch laceration on top of his head. "Does your head hurt?"

"Yes."

"Well, it should. You took quite a lick when you dove into the creek, Sparky." She glanced at Joey. "Could you please hold this cloth against you brother's head while I check out a few things."

Nodding, Joey wiped his wet face with the back of his forearm, then reached for the shirt.

"Not too tightly," Amy instructed. "Just enough to stop the blood flow."

Palms resting on her thighs, Amy leaned over Timmy, looking deep into his eyes. "Okay, Sparky, I need to ask you a few questions."

"My name ain't 'Sparky.' "

Amy quirked a brow. "Oh? It's not?" She emphatically rolled her eyes. "Right. Hal called you 'Buddy.' That must be it."

"No. It's Timmy. T-I-M-M-Y."

"Are you sure about that?"

"I'm sure."

Thank God, Amy thought. He was coherent. "Nice to meet you, Timmy, although, I would have preferred we got to know each other under different circumstances. I need to check you out before we move you. First I'm going to check your eyes. Okay?"

" 'Kay."

She bent so that she was practically nose to nose with the child, cupping her hand over one of his eyes, then pulling it quickly away, checking for proper dilation and contraction of the pupils. A darkened room and an ophthalmoscope would have been much better, but she had to do the best she could with what was available. Satisfied his eyes were both functioning properly, she proceeded to check for feeling in his arms and legs. He had equal strength in his hands when she asked him to squeeze her fingers, and he indicated he felt her brush her fingertips across his palms, his legs, and the bottom of his feet. She found nothing in the examination indicating he shouldn't be moved. Yet, something didn't feel right. Something in the pit of her stomach told her to proceed with extreme caution.

Setting back on her heels, she muttered half to Hal, half to herself, "Everything checks out all right."

"Good. I'll carry him to the car." He leaned forward and started to pick up Timmy, and Amy almost let him. But, just before Hal slipped him arms beneath the child's knees and shoulders, she placed a hand on his forearm, stopping him. He met her gaze.

"I don't think we should move him," she said.

Hal studied her face a few seconds. They both knew they could get Timmy to the clinic faster than the EMTs could get to that area on the creek and transport the boy. But Amy couldn't quell the sixth sense warning her not to move him.

"Okay," Hal agreed, sitting back on his heels.

"There's a cell phone in my purse," she told him. "I need you to call the ambulance service. You'll need to hit the 'send' button twice after dialing the number."

Hal nodded and started to rise. Before he could, Amy remembered Cedar Creek had only one ambulance and grabbed his arm again. "Hal, if the EMTs are tied up, find a flat board big and strong enough to support Timmy, and a thick towel so I can brace his neck. Then call Robert and tell him to meet us at the clinic ASAP. Krista and Joey can stay here with me."

"Got it, Doc." With that, he leaned over, planted a quick kiss on her mouth, then jumped up and trotted away.

The warmth of his lips lingered on hers, even after he disappeared from sight. But she had little time to consider what the intimate gesture meant or where it would lead.

Because right now, she had a patient to see to.

thirteen

Forty-five minutes later, Hal, Joey, and Krista sat waiting in the clinic's reception area while Amy and Robert treated and assessed Timmy's injuries.

After five minutes of solemn silence, Joey asked in a small voice, "Hal, is Timmy going to die?"

Hal looked over at the boy, whose eyes swam with worry. The child's knuckle-white hands were clasped in his lap, and his bare feet dangled a couple of inches above the clinic's white tiled floor. A colorful beach towel Hal had retrieved from his SUV was about to slip from the boy's shoulders.

"No, Joey, Timmy's not going to die," Hal said, adjusting the towel. "But, he may have some serious injuries."

Joey's chin quivered. "I didn't mean for him to get hurt. I just dared him because he's such a wimp most the time. I didn't think he'd really do it."

Aw, man, thought Hal. He wished Joey's mother would hurry up and get there. Hal's parenting skills were limited to his five-year-old tomboy. What did one say to an adolescent boy consumed with guilt over his younger brother's injuries? Both kids knew better than to sneak down to the creek alone and without their mother's permission. Hal didn't want to excuse their disobedience, but, at the same time, he didn't want to make Joey feel worse.

Hal leaned forward, elbows on knees, rubbing his palms together as he gathered his thoughts. "You know, Joey, when we do something we know is wrong, we might get by with it once, maybe even twice. But, eventually, disobedience will result in unpleasant consequences, like it did today. You and Timmy disobeyed your mom and the result was an accident that hurt Timmy."

141

A tear slipped from the inner corner of Joey's eye. He ducked his head. "I'm sorry, Hal. I didn't mean for it to happen."

"I don't want you to feel the fault's all yours, Joey. You and Timmy both knew better than to slip down to the creek alone. Besides, if you let Timmy know you think this is all your fault, he'll have you waiting on him hand and foot the rest of your life. Now, you don't want that, do you?"

Joey looked back up at Hal, the corner of his mouth twitching in a teary smile. "No."

The boy's weepy grin lifted Hal's spirits a bit. "Let this be a lesson to you," he said. "Never go down to the creek again without your mom's permission and never *ever* go swimming without adult supervision. Got that?"

Joey nodded.

Hal gave Joey a playful elbow-to-shoulder shove. "I'm proud of you. If you hadn't pulled Timmy out of the water, he would have drowned for sure."

Joey's spine straightened a bit. Sniffing, he wiped his nose with the back of his hand then lifted one shoulder in a seemingly nonchalant shrug. "Just did what I had to do."

Hal detected a note of pride in the boy's voice and couldn't help smiling. "Well, you did good," he said, giving Joey's shoulder another playful shove.

The front door swished open and a petite woman with short brown hair and a multitude of freckles sailed into the waiting room. "Joey, Hal, where's Timmy?"

Hal stood and gently captured Maggie Brown's upper arms. "Timmy's with the doctors," he told her. "He had a cut on his head that needed stitches and they were going to check him out for other possible injuries."

She looked up at Hal through dark brown eyes rounded with a mixture of fear and worry. "Is he going to be okay?"

"I think so," was all Hal could tell her. Giving her arms a gentle squeeze, he added, "He's in good hands, Maggie. He's got the best with him right now."

"You're right. Robert is the best."

In her concern for her child, she'd apparently missed the information contained in Hal's words when he'd told her Timmy was in with the *doctors*. Hal was about to explain that Robert had some very reliable help when the door leading to the examination area opened and Amy stepped through it.

She paused, her eyes quickly scanning the four people in the waiting room, then her gaze settled on Maggie. "You must be Timmy's mom."

Hal dropped his hands from Maggie's arms as she turned to face Amy. "Yes, I am," Maggie said. "Are you the nurse?"

Amy didn't seem at all offended. She simply stepped forward and offered her right hand to Maggie. "My name is Amy Jordan." Then, with only the slightest hesitation, she added, "I'm a doctor. A pediatrician."

Maggie took Amy's proffered hand. "I see." Her face registered a fleeting flicker of surprise, then her son's welfare apparently took precedence over all else. "How's Timmy?" she asked, dropping Amy's hand.

"His prognosis is good, Mrs. Brown."

"Oh, thank God!" Tears sprang into the mother's eyes and a trembling hand fluttered to her chest. "When can I see him?"

"I think right now is as good a time as any." Amy captured Maggie's elbow and guided her toward the door. "I think Timmy's pretty anxious to see you, too. Then Robert and I will need to talk to you about treatment."

Joey jumped up from where he'd been quietly sitting. "Can I come, too?"

Amy looked back and offered the boy one of her heart-stopping smiles. "I think little heroes are allowed." She motioned with her head. "Come on." Then she shifted her gaze to Hal. "I'll be back in a minute."

With nothing else left to do, Hal sat back down beside Krista, but his thoughts remained on Amy. How would today's events affect her? Just a few short days ago, she'd told him she blamed herself for a patient's death and could no longer practice medicine. But today, she hadn't been given a choice. Out there on that creek bank, she'd been forced to give a child the medical attention he needed.

On the outside, Hal had seen a doctor in complete control, confident of her every move, administering treatment with a strong and steady hand.

But what about on the inside? When the dust from Timmy's accident settled and Amy had time to think about what had taken place, how would she deal with it? Would she retreat into that shell she had helplessly fallen into after Jessica's death?

Hal refused to believe she would. She was a lot stronger than she gave herself credit for. Plus now, she had God to lean on. . .and Hal. He'd be there for her no matter what. He loved her that much. . .and more.

Fifteen minutes later, Amy strolled back into the waiting room alone.

Hal rose and opened his arms to her. She gracefully stepped into them as though their union was the most natural thing in the world. He wrapped her securely in his embrace in hopes of comforting her, but wondered if he wasn't more on the receiving end. She slipped her arms around his waist and rested her head on his shoulder, then she took a deep breath and exhaled slowly. Her chest rose and fell softly against his.

Hal sighed in contentment. Having her in his arms felt so right, like they were both exactly where they were supposed to be, were born to be.

He drew back so he could see her face. That gorgeous face with the emerald eyes and the full, soft lips. How much more could his poor heart take before he sated himself with a kiss? Not something like that mindless and impulsive peck he'd given her at the creek before he dashed off to find help for Timmy, but a real kiss. He wanted to taste her, savor her, pour his heart and soul into hers, show her how much he cherished her.

But right now, standing in a waiting room while his daughter watched them with curious little eyes was not the time or place.

Tonight, he decided. Tonight he'd tell her how he felt about her, then kiss her until they were both breathless and weak in the knees. Hopefully, his heart would hold out until then.

He tucked her stubborn lock of hair behind her ear. "How's Timmy?"

"It took twelve stitches to sew up that hard head of his. I don't think he's going to like his haircut."

"I'd say right now he's just happy to be alive."

Amy worried her right lower lip, her expression turning serious. "We're transporting him to Lexington."

Surprised, Hal stepped back, but kept his hands on her upper arms. "Why?"

"He has a hairline fracture in his fifth cervical vertebra." Amy demonstrated by lifting a finger to a spot low on the back of her neck. "Right here."

"How serious is that?"

"It could have been very serious, but, like I said, it's hairline and, fortunately, the bone stayed intact. As far as Robert and I can tell, there's no nerve damage. That's why he still has feelings in all extremities.

"We both agreed he needs to see a specialist, and probably spend a few days in the hospital, but, I think he'll be fine once he heals." Her lips tipped. "To be honest, his head will probably give him more grief than his cracked vertebra. That's why he needs to be somewhere the doctors can watch him and keep him still for a while."

Hal ran his hands up and down her arms. "What about you? How are you doing?"

Her smile faded a bit, and her face took on a thoughtful expression. Her penetrating gaze captured his, then slipped beneath the surface to touch that place inside him that now belonged to her.

"I'm fine," she finally said. "Really fine," she repeated with unequivocal conviction.

Hal studied her expression and in it saw a serene glow. Yes, he thought with relief, she really was fine.

He felt a tug at the bottom of his shorts and glanced down to find Krista looking up at him with somber eyes. "Daddy will you hold me now?"

Amy pulled away from him, apparently sensing what he did—that his daughter was feeling left out, perhaps a little jealous of the new woman stepping into her father's life. A spur of panic jabbed at Hal's chest. He hoped this wasn't going to be a problem, because no matter how much he loved Amy, his daughter's happiness had to come first.

He bent and scooped up Krista, hoisting her to his hip and embracing her in an enthusiastic hug. "There's always room in my arms for you, Buttercup."

Krista laid her head on her father's shoulder and peered stoically at Amy for a few seconds. Amy smiled warmly at the child but kept her distance, as though she dared not tread on forbidden territory. Hal felt the bitter hands of disappointment close around his throat. *Dear Lord, please let Krista learn to love Amy as much as I do.*

A few more pensive seconds passed, then Krista extended her hand toward Amy, curling a forefinger to summon the doctor forward. Cautiously, Amy stepped up to Hal and his daughter. Raising her head, Krista curled one arm around Hal's neck and the other arm around Amy's. "I love you, Miss Amy," she said, then brushed a butterfly kiss across Amy's cheek.

Hal's knees almost buckled with relief, but he still somehow found the strength to wrap his arms around his young daughter and the woman of his dreams.

"I love you, too, Krista," Amy said, and returned a kiss to his daughter's cheek.

Oh, this is good, Hal thought. *No, not just good. Wonderful.* He had all his hopes, dreams, and happiness right here in the circle of his arms, and he knew of only one thing that could make it better.

Amy was the first to pull back. Looking down at her bloodied and muddied shirt, she said, "You know, I could really use a shower."

"So could I," Hal agreed. After handing over his shirt to stop Timmy's bleeding, he'd found a clean one in the back of his Blazer and slipped it on. But the day's events had still left him with his own share of sweat, mud, and blood. "Come on. I'll take you home so you can change, and I'll go home and do the same. Then I'll be back at your place around seven. We've got a lot to talk about."

Hal set Krista on her feet, and she immediately slipped one small hand in Hal's and the other into Amy's, establishing her place between her father and the doctor.

With a heavy heart, Amy walked outside with Hal and Krista. Hal was right, she agreed to herself. They did have a lot to talk about. Only, she didn't think he was going to be pleased with what she had to tell him.

৵

Later that evening, Amy lit the two candles she had set on her dining room table. Between the candles stood a vase of roses she'd dashed out to the florist to get. She had offered to cook—something she rarely did, but she made a pretty good beef stroganoff and, fortunately, she'd had the ingredients on hand.

She wanted tonight to be special, a night to remember. She wanted to sit across from Hal and look at him through the candlelight and engrave every detail of his handsome face onto the pages of her memory. She wanted to capture the essence of his generous heart and tuck it away inside the center of her being, so she could carry a part of him with her wherever she went. And she would go. It was inevitable.

A pressing ache rose in her throat. Fate had dealt her a bittersweet blow today. Sweet because Timmy's accident had forced her to accept one solid, unchangeable truth—she was a doctor. Practicing medicine was not just something she did for a living. It was her vocation, her calling. She had known it the second she put her mouth to Timmy's and offered him her breath in hopes of giving him back his life. Known, at that moment, whatever the outcome, she would have done her best.

Like she had with little Jessica Jones that fatal night four months ago.

Amy filtered a sigh and wandered to the bay window, where she looked out at a brilliantly orange sun bowing to kiss a mountaintop in the western sky. She realized now Hal had been right about the events surrounding Jessica's death. Any doctor could have been given that file that night, and he or she would have probably done exactly what Amy did. The lot just happened to fall on her. Now Amy realized God had a reason for that. Had she not been the doctor on call that night, she'd still be in Atlanta, working ruthless hours, trying to climb the ladder of success ahead of the next guy, putting everything else in her life before God.

And while Amy knew she must go back to practicing medicine, she also realized she couldn't do it without God. He was the calm in the midst of her storm, the strength in her weakness.

And he said unto me, My grace is sufficient for thee: for my strength is made perfect in weakness.

She'd read the verse just yesterday and remembered pausing to ponder the words, and now she stood in awe of their meaning. In her weakness, she'd found the source of her strength. That was one sweet comfort she could take with her as she stepped back into the world of medicine.

The bitter was that her return to practicing medicine meant she would have to leave the man and child she had fallen in love with. Cedar Creek already had one doctor—an excellent one. Amy didn't think the sleepy little town was quite big enough for two. Even if she went into practice in one of the nearby larger towns, she knew firsthand the sacrifices forced upon a doctor's family. She'd never ask that of Hal and Krista.

She shifted her weight and leaned a shoulder against the window frame. Tonight, she would be with Hal. Perhaps, if fate would allow, she'd hold him in her arms once more.

And then. . .?

Tears blurred the sun's orange blaze. Then, she would

break his heart. That thought hurt worse than the breaking of her own.

The doorbell rang. Amy blinked away the moisture and checked the table one last time to make sure everything was in place. Then, pulling back her shoulders and drawing in a deep breath, she went to answer the door.

&

When Amy opened the door, she took Hal's breath away. She was beyond beautiful. She wore a sleeveless teal dress, belted at her tiny waist, with a full skirt that whispered around her ankles. A rosy blush touched her cheeks and her lips shimmered with pink gloss. And, for the first time since he'd met her, her hair was down. Those glorious tresses hung in soft curves around her shoulders and shone like a golden halo under the foyer light. His hands itched to touch it, test its silkiness between his fingertips.

Later, he reminded himself. He wanted to woo her in little by little, show her he knew how to treat her just like the lady she was.

"Come in." She said with a radiant smile.

As he stepped over the threshold, the hearty scent of stewed beef greeted him, but her own elegant scent slipped past the cuisine's aroma and coiled around his senses, drawing him into a heady dream with her at center stage. He stuffed his hands in his pockets to keep from reaching for her.

She led him into the dining room, where he found the table draped in white linen and bathed in candlelight with a crystal vase of six red roses for a centerpiece. He released a silent sigh of contentment. Tonight was going to be perfect. Just perfect.

During the meal they engaged in small talk, and thirty minutes later, Hal pushed away an empty plate and folded his arms on the table. "That was delicious."

"Thank you," she said quietly. Come to think of it, she had been quieter than usual since his arrival. He had done most of the talking. She'd pushed her plate away several minutes ago, having eaten very little, and, Hal noticed, her eyes looked tired.

Perhaps it was the excitement of the day catching up with her.

"Are you okay?" he asked.

"Yes." She sat up a little straighter and sent him a smile that seemed forced. "I was, um. . .just thinking about Timmy."

"Have you heard from him since we left the clinic?"

"I called the hospital in Lexington about an hour ago. He had arrived and they were headed to X-ray with him."

"Tell me something, Amy. When you were examining Timmy at the creek, did you find anything to indicate his neck might be broken?"

Leaning on her forearms, she clasped her hands. "No, I didn't."

"Then, how did you know not to move him?"

She focused on a candle for a moment, the reflection of the flame dancing in her eyes, then looked back at him. "It's hard to explain, really. There are times when I'm examining a patient that I get this feeling"—she pressed a fist against her diaphragm—"right here. It's like a sixth sense telling me what I should or should not do."

"Gut instinct?" Hal guessed.

One corner of her mouth tipped. "Yes. Gut instinct. I know that sounds crazy, but—"

"No, it doesn't. I get the same feeling sometimes when I'm talking to God. It's like He nudges me in the right direction whenever I'm in doubt or confused about something."

She cast her eyes downward. "I know what you mean. I've been experiencing a little of that lately myself."

He reached over with one hand and laced his fingers through hers, willing her to look back up at him. When she did, he said, "You say that like it's a bad thing."

With her free hand, she brushed a lock of silky hair over her shoulder. "I didn't mean to. I'm just. . ." She paused, worried her right lower lip, then smiled. "I'm glad you came tonight, Hal. It means a lot to me."

"Me, too." He squeezed her hand. "Why don't we move this conversation to the living room?"

She merely nodded.

He circled the table and held her chair while she rose, then followed her into the living room. Her steps slowed and stopped in the center of the room, and she just stood there with her pencil-straight back to him for a long moment. What was she thinking? Surely she sensed things were about to change between them. Destiny had been leading them this way from the moment they met.

Finally, she turned and looked at him, and his world spun out of control. Every enamored emotion he had held at bay since the moment he first found her, unconscious, on the side of the road, rushed forward and crashed head-on in the center of his chest. His heart pounded with such fury, he thought it would burst right through his rib cage and fall at her feet.

Now. It had to be now.

"I love you, Amy." His racing heart slowed a bit, like the release of those four small words was just what it needed to calm its erratic beat.

He held his breath while he waited for her reaction.

For what seemed like an eternity, she stood statue still, her expression stoic, her body rigid. Then, tears rose in her eyes and she began to tremble.

A dark hand of foreboding reached inside Hal and pulled the plug on his rising tide of happiness. Somehow, he knew the moisture pooling on her lower lids was not tears of joy.

"I love you, too, Hal." Her soft voice was brimming with pain.

Hal stepped forward, raised his hands and slid his palms up and down her upper arms. Her heart was breaking. He could see it in her face, in the tear that escaped from the corner of her eye. "Tell me what's wrong, Amy."

Wetting her lips, she swallowed. "I'm leaving Cedar Creek."

His hands stopped moving and he just stared at her, wondering if he had heard correctly. "Leaving?" he finally managed to ask.

"Yes."

No!

The silent scream ripped through his veins. This was not happening, Hal told himself. He was merely having a bad dream. He'd fallen asleep in his easy chair at home and would soon wake up, rush to Amy's house, find her table dressed in white linen and candlelight, sweep her into his arms, and tell her he loved her. And that would be that. Fifty years from now, they'd be sitting on their front porch swing holding hands while watching their great-grandchildren play in the yard.

But the burning ache rising in his chest told him he wasn't having a dream. He was wide awake and being catapulted into a living nightmare.

She raised a palm to his cheek. "I'm sorry, Hal."

Sorry? She tells me she loves me but she's leaving in almost the same breath, and all she can say is "I'm sorry"? He grasped her hand and pulled it down to his chest. "May I ask why you're leaving?" His voice rang bitter with frustration, but he couldn't help it. Her leaving had not been in his plans.

"I'm going back into practice."

Somewhere amid the disillusionment and confusion dousing his hopes and dreams, a spark of jubilation ignited. He framed her face with desperate hands. "Amy, that's great. No one could be happier for you than me, because no one could love you more than I do. You're a wonderful doctor and have a lot to offer others. But, why can't you practice in Cedar Creek?"

"Oh, Hal. I wish that were possible. But Cedar Creek already has a doctor. I don't think the town can support two. Besides, if I opened a practice here, it would be like going into competition with Robert, and I could never do that to him. He's been too good of a friend to me."

"You know he wouldn't look at it that way."

"You're right, he probably wouldn't. But I'd have to live with myself."

Hal searched for another argument, but couldn't find one. His mind had gone numb, his legs felt like they'd been chopped off at the knees. He slid his hands to her shoulders. "When?"

he wanted to know.

"I promised Robert and Linda I'd stay until after the baby was born. Two months, three at the most."

"What do we do till then?"

"Nothing."

"Nothing?" He shook his head in indignant disbelief. "Tell me how I'm supposed to live this close to you, in the same town with you, feeling the way I do about you and do nothing about it."

Her eyes brimmed with sad acceptance. "Hal, we have to think of Krista."

Ice water splashed in his face couldn't have jolted his senses more. She was right. He couldn't bring her into his daughter's life knowing their time together would be limited. In the end, it'd break his little girl's heart.

Hal dropped his hands and stepped back. He felt cold and empty, which was probably good. Because when the numbness wore off and the pain set in, he didn't know how he would bear it.

He raked a hapless hand through his hair, trying to collect his wits enough to figure out what he should do next. "Well, I guess that's it, then," he finally managed to say. "I should be going."

He took one last look at Amy, standing in the middle of the living room, her arms crossed, her eyes now dry but her face still streaked with tears. Oh, how his arms ached to hold her, his hands longed to touch her. But it wasn't meant to be. She'd been no more than a beautiful dream after all.

He drew in a deep, painful breath of resignation. She'd done the right thing in ending it now, before his daughter got hurt. A small part of him had to be grateful to Amy for that.

He crammed his hands into his pockets. "I. . .uh. . .guess I'll see you around."

"Yes," she whispered, like a single breath of air was all she had left.

A suffocating sensation pressed on his chest, overwhelmed

him. He had to get out now, while he still had the strength. "I'll see myself out." With that, he turned and walked to the front door on unsteady legs, then he wandered to his car like an aimless drunk, putting one wobbly foot in front of the other until he reached his destination, then wondered how in the world how he'd gotten there.

He opened the car door, but stopped short of getting in and gritted his teeth. *How dare she.* His grip on the door handle tightened to knuckle-white. Anger coiled inside him like a boxer's fist, pushing upward until he saw red. *How dare she tell me she loves me then dash my hopes like they were thin bubbles floating on the air! If she is so bent on leaving, fine. But, by Ned, I'll give her something to remember me by.*

He slammed the car door and marched back up the sidewalk. Without bothering to knock, he opened the door and sailed through it.

"Amy!"

In an instant she stepped from the living room, her already tear-dampened eyes wide with question. "Did you forget something?"

"Yeah." He strolled forward, pulled her into his arms, and covered her mouth with his with all the finesse of a hungry lion.

At first, she was too shocked to do anything and just stood there, her eyes wide and her body rigid. Undaunted, he deepened the kiss, unleashing all his anger and frustration on her soft pliant lips.

When he felt her arms circle his neck and her body go soft against his, a moan of release escaped his throat. He slid his hand up her spine and buried his hand in her hair, curled his fingers around its silky softness.

The kiss turned tender, seeking, like two desert dwellers drinking from a well about to go dry, greedily savoring every pure sweet drop. They may not have each other, but at least they'd have this. This kiss, this memory.

When Hal's lungs were about to explode, he pulled back

and studied her face, her eyes, her mouth, so he could lock every detail of her away in his dreams. Because he knew, with certainty, no woman would ever fill them the way Amy did.

She looked at him through misty eyes full of question and bewilderment. "Hal, I—"

He pressed a finger to her lips. "Gut instinct," he said, then turned and walked away.

fourteen

"Amy?" The receptionist's voice filtered through Amy's telephone intercom.

With her gaze fixed on her computer screen, Amy absent-mindedly reached over with one hand and pressed a button, leaving the other hand on the keyboard. "Yes."

"You have a call on line two."

"Thank you." Amy pulled her gaze away from the screen long enough to pick up the receiver, target the blinking button and punch it, then, sandwiching the receiver between her ear and shoulder, she turned her attention back to the monitor. "Amy Jordan. May I help you?"

"Hello, Sweetheart."

Amy straightened her spine, barely catching the handset before it slipped from her shoulder. "Dad?"

"How are you doing?"

"Fine," she said a bit too quickly. Actually, she was shocked. Since she'd rededicated her life to Christ, she'd phoned her father twice. The first conversation had been a bit stilted, like two strangers sharing a bus seat and searching for something to say to break the monotony of their journey. The second had been a little easier, more like old friends trying to catch up after a long separation. But this was the first time since she'd moved to Cedar Creek that he'd called her. There had to be a reason.

"Is everything okay, Dad?"

"Yes," came his quick reply. "Everything's fine. I was just. . ." He cleared his throat. "I was just thinking about you."

And I've been praying for you she wanted to say, but didn't. She didn't want to push. If they were ever to have a congenial father-daughter relationship, it would have to be in God's time. All Amy had felt led to do so far was reach out to her father. And pray.

Amy swiveled away from her computer and propped an elbow on her desk. "I've been thinking about you a lot lately, too, Dad."

"Yes, ah, well. . ."

Amusement tipped Amy's lips. Engaging in personal conversation made Nicholas Jordan as comfortable as a novice public speaker delivering his first speech. But her father was trying and, with time, he'd get better at it. She was sure.

"I'm taking a couple of days off week after next," he continued. "I thought I'd fly up your way. You know. . ."

Amy could almost see him shrugging one shoulder, almost hear him jangle the keys in his pocket. Character traits she somehow remembered even though they'd spent so little time together.

"Spend some time with you," he finished.

Amy smiled her first heartfelt smile in three weeks. That's how long it'd been since Hal had walked into her house, kissed her senseless, then walked back out the door. . .out of her life.

Thoughts of Hal brought a lump to her throat. Swallowing the knot, she said, "That would be nice, Dad."

They talked on a few more minutes, then Amy hung up the phone with an imminent sense of peace. She and her father were finally connecting, communicating after a lifetime of alienation. It made her wonder what would have happened if she had reached out to him sooner.

She released a despondent sigh. At least something was going right in her life. She stood and wandered to the window. For almost three weeks now, in a desperate attempt to stay close to Hal and Krista, Amy had searched—and prayed—for a nearby town that needed a pediatrician. Maybe a small community within reasonable commuting distance where she could put in a satisfying day's work and still have time for Hal and Krista. . .

A place like Cedar Creek.

But every inquiry she'd made, she'd met with a dead end.

Resting her forehead against the cool windowpane, she looked out at the rugged Cumberland Gap Mountains, christened by a kaleidoscope of fall color: golds, oranges, and reds. And at the foot of those mountains the tiny town of Cedar Creek lay like a precious jewel cradled in her majesty's lap.

A reminiscent smile touched Amy's lips. Just a few short weeks ago this charming little community with its friendly but wary population and its solitary grocery store had felt like a strange and foreign country to her. Now, it held a special and permanent place inside her, just like Hal and Krista.

Her smile faded as a dull ache rose in her chest. Hal and Krista. How would she ever live without them?

Her chin quivered. She pursed her lips. *Accept it, Amy,* she told herself. *It just wasn't meant to be.*

A shuddery sigh left her chest. Deep down, she knew she would be all right. God was big enough and strong enough to fill the gaping wound in her heart. And somehow, some way, she and Hal would both move on. Someday they'd be able to look back on the short time they'd had together as a fond and cherished memory.

Amy had told herself that countless times over the past three weeks. And she'd pretty much made up her mind that was how things must be. She would leave Cedar Creek. It was God's will.

Now, all she had to do was convince her heart.

a

Much later that day, Amy was reorganizing a file cabinet when a knock sounded on her office door. "Come in," she called in response.

The door opened and Robert stepped inside, frowning when he saw her. "You don't look so good."

She closed the file drawer a little harder than intended. "You and Linda are the only two people in the world who could get away with telling me that."

He strolled to her desk, pulled out one of the guest chairs, and sat down. "We're worried about you. You look like you haven't slept or eaten in days."

She hadn't. Not much, anyway. And her weariness and loneliness were apparently beginning to show.

Drawing back her shoulders, she ambled to her desk. "I'm fine, Robert." She pulled out her chair and sank down. "I'm just a little tired. That's all."

"Then why are you still here? The office closed over an hour ago."

Just trying to stay busy, she thought. *Trying to keep my mind occupied and my brain busy so I can get through another day without Hal's presence in my life.*

Oh, she had seen him a few times, around town and at church. But the encounters had been awkward, like two bad actors in an amateur play, forgetting their lines and bungling through a lousy ad lib. And the meetings always managed to leave her missing him more than if she hadn't seen him at all.

How was she going to survive living in this town two more months, looking for him around every corner, seeing him from time to time, but never able to reach out and touch him, or satisfy her need to hold him?

"Amy?"

She blinked, snapping back to the here and now. "Yes?"

"Didn't you hear me?"

Yes, she'd heard him. But what had he said? She searched her short-term memory and came up empty. "I'm sorry, Robert. My mind strayed. What was it you said?"

"I said if you're tired, why are you still here? The office closed an hour ago."

"Oh." She hesitated, searching her mind for an excuse. She couldn't tell him the real reason she was spending so much time at work. "I'm just trying to catch up," she finally said.

"By cleaning out a file cabinet you organized less than two months ago? I don't think so."

She hunched one shoulder. "Has to be done some time."

A brief silence fell between them, and an instinctive knot twisted in Amy's stomach. Somehow she knew where Robert was headed with the conversation, and she didn't want to go there.

But before she could change his direction, he said, "I saw Hal yesterday."

A smothery feeling rose in her chest. Dropping her gaze, she thumbed a stack of outgoing mail. "That's nice," she muttered as nonchalantly as she could manage, hoping she sounded more convincing to Robert than she did to herself. "How are he, his mom, and Krista doing?"

"I imagine Krista and Ellen are doing fine, but Hal looks as miserable as you."

Her busy hands stilled. She raised her lashes, meeting his smug expression with an irritated scowl. "Just what makes you think you know so much about Hal and me?"

A knowing grin curved his lips. "I may be a busy man, Amy, but I've got eyes." With a forefinger, he tapped the rim of his glasses. "Twenty-twenty with these babies. And I think I know my two best friends pretty well. You two were headed down lover's lane just a few weeks ago. Now, whenever you meet, it's like two porcupines passing each other in a drain pipe."

She didn't argue. What was the point? Robert pretty much had her pegged.

Leaning on her forearms, she clasped her hands tightly. "I really don't want to talk about Hal," she said past the catch in her throat. "We do need to talk about my job here, though." Robert had been so busy at the clinic lately that she hadn't had a chance to talk to him about her plans to leave after Linda had the baby. But since he was here now, sitting at her desk and obviously in a talking mood, she figured she'd better seize the opportunity so he could be working on her replacement.

He settled back, crossing an ankle over the opposite knee. "You're right," he surprised her by saying. "We do need to talk about your job."

"Is something wrong?" She wouldn't be surprised if he said "Yes." After all, she hadn't been on top of things lately.

"Yes," he said, echoing her thoughts.

With her fingertips, she kneaded her closed eyes, gritty from loss of sleep and tears. "I'm sorry, Robert. I guess I'm just not cut out to be an office manager."

"Boy, I'll say," came his quick reply.

That did it. She was tired and irritable and his impudent response rubbed her the wrong way. Opening her eyes, she dropped her hands to the desktop with a thud and leveled him with a glower. "First you tell me I look horrible, then that I'm doing a poor job. I'm beginning to wonder if I want to keep you as a friend."

He shook his head. "You misunderstand me, Amy. You're doing a wonderful job. But you don't belong in here behind a desk. You belong out there,"—he pointed a thumb over his shoulder—"with your patients."

Propping her chin in her hand, she released a weary sigh. "I know."

Surprise jerked his head back a couple of inches. "You do?"

Her lips tipped. "Yes, I do." She went on to tell him how her experience with Timmy and her newfound faith in God had given her the courage to return to practicing medicine. By the time she finished, he was all smiles.

Sitting back, he pushed his glasses up the bridge of his nose. "Good. Now you can come into practice with me."

This time, it was she who yanked her head back in surprise. "You can't be serious."

"On the contrary, Dr. Jordan. I am *very* serious."

As she studied his zealous expression, suspicion crept in. "Has Hal been talking to you?"

Robert's brow dipped in confusion. "About what?"

"About my going into practice with you."

"Why would he?"

"To keep me in Cedar Creek."

"Oh." Robert nodded in understanding, then shook his head

in denial. "No. Hal hasn't said anything to me about you."

She glanced away in order to mask her disappointment. "Good. Because I don't need any favors. I can always go back to Atlanta to practice." Looking back at him, she added, "The senior partners at Mercy told me I had a place there if I ever decided to go back."

He raked his fingers through his thick, brown hair. An unruly lock fell across his forehead. "At the risk of sounding selfish, I'm not offering you a partnership so much as a favor to you as I am a favor to myself."

She scrutinized him a moment, wondering about the truth in his statement. She knew he *would* offer her a partnership as a favor to her, just as he knew she would *never* accept a handout. But the earnestness in his eyes and the sincerity on his face told her he was being honest with her, and a thin thread of hope wove through her.

Still, she had to be sure. "Robert, you always manage to see all the patients. How would I be doing you a favor by taking half of that away from you?"

Settling back in his seat, he laced his hands over his flat stomach. "Amy, one of the reasons I came to Cedar Creek is because I didn't want to get caught in the same trap our fathers did. Working night and day and having nothing left over to give my family. But lately, that's exactly what I've been doing. I knew when I came here it would take a while to earn the community's trust, but it looks like I finally have. More and more patients are coming to the clinic rather than driving to a neighboring town to see a doctor like they once had to do, and I'm having to work like crazy to see them all.

"Right now it's"—he checked his watch—"six o'clock. This is the first time in weeks I've finished up before seven. Not to mention the three emergency calls I received in the middle of the night this week. And, no offense to you, but I'd much rather be home right now, cuddling with my pregnant wife, than sitting here trying to persuade you to go into practice with me. But I know this discussion is necessary. The sooner I can convince you how much you're needed here, the better for the both of us."

Amy sat in shocked silence. Was she dreaming? Or was this a splendid reality?

A prayer answered?

Her mind spun with confusion. She pressed her fingers to her temples. "Robert, I don't know what to say."

"Say 'Yes.' " When she didn't immediately, he once again leaned forward, folding his arms on his desk. "Think about it, Amy. I'm a family practitioner; you're a pediatrician. I'll see the adults; you'll see the children. The balance would be perfect. This town is small enough and the patients few enough that we could both put in a satisfying day's work and still have time to spend with our families."

His features softened. "Amy, I want to have time to hold my daughter when she gets here, rock her to sleep, even change a diaper or two. I want to go to bed at night and hold my wife when I'm not so tired I'm asleep before my head hits the pillow.

"And you, Amy. I know you. If you go back to Mercy, you'll end up meeting everyone else's needs but your own. If you stay here, you can pour yourself into your work and still have time to watch Krista grow. You can be there for Hal when he's put in a hard day at work, and vice versa."

In her mind, Amy repeated Robert's list of reasons for her to accept his offer.

Pour herself into her work.

Watch Krista grow.

Be there for Hal.

Everything she wanted. Exactly what she'd prayed for.

The shadows lifted from her heart and the confusion vanished from her mind. No wonder she hadn't been able to find a nearby town to practice in. God already had a place picked out for her, right here in Cedar Creek.

Robert leaned back. "If you want to take a few days to think about my offer, then, of course, I understand."

A few days? She didn't even need a few minutes. "I have only one question for you," she said.

"What's that?"

"When do I start?"

A huge grin split Robert's face. "How about Monday? We'll shuffle the paperwork between us until we find another office manager."

"Great." She grabbed her purse from her bottom desk drawer, jumped up, and flitted around her desk like a hummingbird. Bending down, she planted a sisterly kiss on Robert's cheek. "Lock up for me, will you?" With that, she headed for the door.

"Hey, where are you going in such a hurry?"

Without breaking her stride, she glanced back. "To see Hal, of course."

❧

When Amy knocked on the door, Ellen Cooper opened it. "Oh, Amy, dear, I am so glad to see you." She captured Amy's upper arm and pulled her inside. "Our woodshed is overflowing."

"Pardon?" Amy said, not having the vaguest idea what the older woman was talking about.

Ellen fanned a hand through the air. "Never mind. Hal's out back. Follow me." She led Amy through the foyer and living room, stopping at the French doors leading out onto the patio.

Beyond the door's clear panes, Amy saw him. Ax in hand, he stood next to a woodpile at the far edge of the backyard, his sinewy, sweat-dampened back glistening in the setting sun. Drawn by the mesmerizing spell he always cast over her, Amy inched forward until her breath painted a small foggy circle on the glass.

With his free hand, he withdrew a log from the woodpile and set it end-up on a large stump, then he raised the ax over his head and brought it down with whiplash force. The log split, the two halves launching in opposite directions. He bent, picking up the half nearest him and stood it upright on the stump.

"Well," Ellen said from where she stood beside Amy, "I'll

let you take it from here." Then, shaking her head, the older woman walked away muttering, "That boy never could keep his shirt on."

Amy opened the door and slipped outside, but didn't leave the patio; she just stood watching the finest specimen of a man she'd ever laid eyes on. And he loved her.

For a split instant, her mind spun to her old life, and what she was leaving behind. She'd experienced the glitter and glamour of city life, rubbed shoulders with some of the world's most renowned doctors, known the privileges wealth could buy. But all that paled when compared to what lay ahead of her—the love of an honorable man and faith in a God who would never forsake her.

A window of revelation opened up to her and words from the popular twenty-third Psalm poured from her memory.

He leadeth me beside the still waters. He restoreth my soul.

Her entire being overflowed with peace, filling her joy cup to the brim. Truly, when God led her to a sleepy little town called Cedar Creek, He had led her to still waters—and restored her soul.

Hal started to raise the ax once more, then, as though sensing her presence, twisted his upper body around. Their gazes locked, and at least a dozen giddy butterflies took flight in Amy's stomach. She felt like she was about to step into the happy ending of a fairy tale.

Without taking his eyes off her, he laid aside the ax and reached for a shirt draped across the back of a nearby lawn chair.

Simultaneously, they started toward each other, he fastening buttons, and she so light on her feet, she barely felt the ground beneath her. They stopped with less than a foot separating them and stood looking at each other for a moment in silence.

Dark circles ringed his eyes, and his face appeared thinner. Had he lost weight?

Regret pressed down upon her. Whatever made her think

she could leave him?

"Hi," he finally said.

"Hi."

His gaze roamed her face. "You look good."

Liar, she thought. "Thank you," she said aloud. "You don't."

Shaking his head, he released a halfhearted chuckle. "You never cease to amaze me, Doc." Then his spiritless joviality faded. "I was going to call you tonight."

She arched her brows. "You were?"

"Yeah." He nodded. "I wanted to come over and talk to you."

"Oh? What about?"

He slipped his fingers into his jeans' pockets. "I've been thinking. About us." He glanced away for a few seconds, as though considering his next words, then looked back to her. "You know, if you practiced somewhere like Lexington, we could move halfway between here and there. At the most, each of us would only have an hour's commute."

So, he'd come up with a plan for them to be together. She almost laughed out loud with delight. He wasn't any more willing to let her go than she was willing to lose him. Feeling a bit impish, she crossed her arms. "You think that would work?"

"I think we could make it work. Don't you?"

She cocked her head to one side. "What if I don't want to practice in Lexington?"

His shoulders drooped. "Then Krista and I will go with you wherever you want to go."

Tears burned the back of her throat. "You'd do that for me?"

He raised his hand to her upper arms and rubbed up and down. "Amy, I'd do anything for you. I don't particularly want to leave Cedar Creek. But, I'd do it before losing you."

Amy would have never thought it possible, but at that moment, her love for him grew. Heart overflowing, she lifted her hands to his face, reveling in the prickly feel of his day-old beard beneath her palms. The windows of heaven seemed to open and flood her soul with liquid sunshine. She loved this man. Oh, how she loved him.

"What if I were to tell you I've been doing some thinking of my own," she said, "and I've come up with a way we can be together without leaving Cedar Creek?"

The rise and fall of his chest intensified. "I'd be interested in hearing it."

She let her hands fall to his chest, just to feel his rapid heartbeat keeping time with her own. "What if I were to tell you Robert's offered me a partnership in his practice, and I accepted?"

The pulsing beneath her fingertips quickened even more. "You did?" he asked, sounding like a kid afraid of getting his hopes up.

"Of course, Silly. Why should we live halfway between here and anywhere else when we don't have to?"

She felt his arms circle her waist and saw hope rise in his eyes. "Tell me this is real, Doc. Tell me I'm not dreaming."

A coy smile tipped her lips as she slid her arms around his neck. "Why don't I just show you?" She pulled him close and kissed him, telling him with her heart what she knew he wanted to hear. When she drew back, she said, "Well, what do you think? Dream or reality?"

He pulled her back into the circle his arms, tipping his head toward hers. "I don't know," he said with a rakish grin. "I haven't made my mind up yet."

epilogue

Five Months Later

Outside the Cooper home, a frigid March wind sliced through the crisp evening air. But inside, all was warm and cozy.

An inviting fire popped and crackled in the fireplace. In a rocking chair flanking the hearth, Ellen sat, reading glasses perched on the end of her nose. Her agile hands skillfully worked her knitting needles, building stitches on what would soon be a new afghan for Krista's bed.

On the sofa, between Hal and Amy, Krista sat with her rosy cheek resting against Amy's upper arm, listening while Amy read the story of Hannah and Samuel. Amy paused a moment and glanced over at her husband. He sat with his legs stretched out and crossed at the ankles, his hand clasped over his abdomen, his head laid back on the top of the sofa. His chest rose and fell with the steady rhythm of slumber.

Poor guy. He'd had such a hard day at work. She felt an overwhelming need to reach over and brush the back of her fingers across his jaw.

"Tell me what happens next, Mama."

Krista's voice penetrated Amy's thoughts, and she continued with the story.

The four months Amy had been married to Hal had been the best of her life. The immense pleasure she found in simple things—the feel of Krista's hand in hers, a quiet evening spent with her new family, hearing Hal say "I love you" every day—never ceased to amaze her.

Only one thing could make her life more complete, and she'd see what Hal had to say about it later on tonight.

"So," she continued, finishing the story, "God gave Hannah

a son, and Hannah named the child Samuel."

She looked down at Krista, who stared at the book, her lips pursed, one corner of her mouth tucked in. Amy knew that expression well. It meant her daughter was doing some heavy thinking.

After half a minute of thoughtful silence, Krista glanced up at Amy. "Do you think if I pray for a baby brother, God will give me one?"

Before Amy could respond, Hal snapped to attention, opening his eyes and sitting up straight. "Okay, Buttercup," he said. "Time for you to go to bed."

Amy grinned. Her husband hadn't been sleeping after all.

Later, while Amy sat at the dresser in her and Hal's bedroom, brushing her hair, he came in, closing and locking the door behind him. A giddy flutter of anticipation fluttered in her chest.

He stepped up behind her and, with his gentle, work-roughened hands, started kneading her shoulders. "So, my beautiful wife, I finally have you all to myself."

Laying aside the brush, Amy rested the back of her head against his abdomen, meeting his reflected gaze in the mirror. "I love you, Hal."

A lazy half smile touched his lips. "I love you, too, Dr. Cooper."

Sweeping aside her hair, he leaned down and pressed a whisper-soft kiss just below her ear. Gooseflesh raced over her body, but she resisted the desire to turn into the embrace she knew awaited her. She had something to tell her husband, and if she didn't do so now, she'd never get to it tonight.

"Hal?"

"Mmmm?" he responding, still raining kisses on her neck.

"Do you think Krista will be disappointed if God gives her a baby sister instead of a baby brother?"

He mumbled something that sounded like "Don't know."

Amy's shoulders drooped. She rolled her eyes. "Honey, you're not listening to me."

He raised his head, looking at her mirrored reflection with a confused and somewhat impatient frown marring his forehead. "Do we have to talk about this now?"

"Better now than when he or she gets here. . .don't you think?"

Amy watched while Hal's disgruntled expression change to one of wonder. "Exactly what are you saying, Sweetheart?"

"That come November, Krista should get her wish. That is, if it's a boy."

Hal blinked. "You mean. . .?"

Amy nodded.

He kneeled, turning her around to face him. Mixed emotions played across his face—awe, amazement, unquestionable love. He laid his palm on her flat stomach. She covered his hand with her own.

"Wow," he whispered, as though he could already feel the baby kicking.

"Yes," she whispered back. "Wow."

Hal closed the distance between him and his wife, a tear of joy in his eye and a prayer of thanksgiving in his heart.

A Letter To Our Readers

Dear Reader:

In order that we might better contribute to your reading enjoyment, we would appreciate your taking a few minutes to respond to the following questions. We welcome your comments and read each form and letter we receive. When completed, please return to the following:

Rebecca Germany, Fiction Editor
Heartsong Presents
PO Box 719
Uhrichsville, Ohio 44683

1. Did you enjoy reading *Still Waters?*
   ☐ Very much. I would like to see more books
      by this author!
   ☐ Moderately
      I would have enjoyed it more if _____

   _____

   _____

2. Are you a member of **Heartsong Presents**? Yes ☐ No ☐
   If no, where did you purchase this book?_____

   _____

3. How would you rate, on a scale from 1 (poor) to 5 (superior),
   the cover design?_____

4. On a scale from 1 (poor) to 10 (superior), please rate the
   following elements.

   _____ Heroine   _____ Plot

   _____ Hero   _____ Inspirational theme

   _____ Setting   _____ Secondary characters

5. These characters were special because_____

_____

_____

6. How has this book inspired your life?_____

_____

_____

7. What settings would you like to see covered in future
    Heartsong Presents books?_____

_____

_____

8. What are some inspirational themes you would like to see
    treated in future books?_____

_____

_____

9. Would you be interested in reading other **Heartsong
    Presents** titles?   Yes ❏   No ❏

10. Please check your age range:
    ❏ Under 18   ❏ 18-24   ❏ 25-34
    ❏ 35-45   ❏ 46-55   ❏ Over 55

11. How many hours per week do you read?_____

Name _____

Occupation _____

Address _____

City _____ State _____ Zip _____

new year, new love

Introducing four brand-new novellas in modern settings that reflect on the anticipation of entering a new year—new calendar, new goals to accomplish, and a new chance at love. Rejoice in the transformation of a young woman in *Remaking Meridith* by Carol Cox. Throughout *Beginnings*, Peggy Darty will have you laughing and crying as two lonely adults are laid up in the hospital over the holiday season. Then, discover how setting goals brings together a church singles' class and sparks the flame of love in *Never Say Never* by Yvonne Lehman. Finally, in *Letters to Timothy*, see how author Pamela Kaye Tracy unites five needy people with one pen pal letter.

paperback, 352 pages, 5 ³⁄₁₆" x 8"

❤ ❤ ❤ ❤ ❤ ❤ ❤ ❤ ❤ ❤ ❤ ❤ ❤ ❤ ❤ ❤

❤ ❤ ❤ ❤ ❤ ❤ ❤ ❤ ❤ ❤ ❤ ❤ ❤ ❤ ❤ ❤

·······Presents·······

Great Inspirational Romance at a Great Price!

Heartsong Presents books are inspirational romances in contemporary and historical settings, designed to give you an enjoyable, spirit-lifting reading experience. You can choose wonderfully written titles from some of today's best authors like Veda Boyd Jones, Yvonne Lehman, Tracie Peterson, Debra White Smith, and many others

When ordering quantities less than twelve, above titles are $2.95 each.
Not all titles may be available at time of order.

Heart♥ng Presents
Love Stories Are Rated G!

That's for godly, gratifying, and of course, great! If you love a thrilling love story, but don't appreciate the sordidness of some popular paperback romances, **Heartsong Presents** is for you. In fact, **Heartsong Presents** is the *only inspirational romance book club* featuring love stories where Christian faith is the primary ingredient in a marriage relationship.

Sign up today to receive your first set of four, never before published Christian romances. Send no money now; you will receive a bill with the first shipment. You may cancel at any time without obligation, and if you aren't completely satisfied with any selection, you may return the books for an immediate refund.

Imagine. . .four new romances every four weeks—two historical, two contemporary—with men and women like you who long to meet the one God has chosen as the love of their lives. .all for the low price of $9.97 postpaid.

To join, simply complete the coupon below and mail to the address provided. **Heartsong Presents** romances are rated G for another reason: They'll arrive *Godspeed!*